THE SEANCE

"Was Mary there the night Jerry died?" Pamela asked finally.

"Pamela," Savey complained. "Now you're being insensitive."

Mary noticed Ken leaning forward. To see the answer.

Ask her.

"We have asked her," Pamela insisted. "She says she was not there."

The Ouija board did not respond.

"Is Mary lying?" Pamela asked.

"This is heavy," Radi said.

You lie. She lies. All lie.

Pamela was annoyed. "It was a nightmare the night Jerry died. We just want to put that nightmare behind us. Can't you answer our questions?"

It did not hesitate.

The nightmare is before you.

Books by Christopher Pike

Available from ARCHWAY Paperbacks

Christopher PIKE

The Visitor

WITHDRAWN

AN ARCHWAY PAPERBACK
Published by POCKET BOOKS
New York   London   Toronto   Sydney   Tokyo   Singapore

This book is a work of fiction. Names, characters, places and incidents are products of the author's imagination or are used fictitiously. Any resemblance to actual events or locales or persons, living or dead, is entirely coincidental.

AN ARCHWAY PAPERBACK *Original*

An Archway Paperback published by
POCKET BOOKS, a division of Simon & Schuster Inc.
1230 Avenue of the Americas, New York, NY 10020

Copyright © 1995 by Christopher Pike

All rights reserved, including the right to reproduce
this book or portions thereof in any form whatsoever.
For information address Pocket Books, 1230 Avenue
of the Americas, New York, NY 10020

ISBN: 0-671-87270-2

First Archway Paperback printing November 1995

10 9 8 7 6 5 4 3 2 1

AN ARCHWAY PAPERBACK and colophon are
registered trademarks of Simon & Schuster Inc.

Cover art by Danilo Ducak

Printed in the U.S.A.

IL 9+

For Caroline Poplak,
my British editor,
whom I adore

Prayer of a False God

All are doomed to burn.
Love feeds the flames.
Days of endless pains.
And the smoke takes each in turn.

All are doomed to rust.
Time destroys our lives.
Nights cut like knives.
And the wind carries away the dust.

All are doomed to love.
All are doomed to die.
Tonight bring the black tomb.
For even the most high.
Even those in this room.
Cannot pretend to fly
And I know.
Even you.
Even I.
Must die.

The Visitor

1

The horror always came with waking. For that reason Mary Weist's vision could not be described as a simple nightmare. The more she pushed toward consciousness, the greater the pain became. This was no dream because it bloomed under the bright sun. The pain came before the memory, small and sharp like shards of ice implanted in her chest. Then, with the recollection of Jerry Rickman, the ice would turn to bubbling acid, and her heart would break.

It would be all she could do not to wake up screaming.

Mary was napping that Friday evening before the big party at Pamela Poole's. Lately she'd been sleeping a great deal. It wasn't uncommon for her to come home from school and lie down for three hours at a stretch. Only a month had gone by since her boyfriend, Jerry, had been shot to death. Her parents saw her chronic fatigue as her way of coping with the crushing grief. But the sleep never refreshed her. Because she always had to go through that somnolent state waking up and wishing she were dead.

That Friday evening was no exception. Once awake, Mary moaned and rolled over in bed. She would have wept if the tears would have helped. But tears were as useless as dreams. Jerry was dead; that was all that mattered.

Eventually Mary got up and began to dress. It was seven-ten, and Savey Barker was supposed to pick her up at eight. In the next room she could hear her parents packing and talking quietly. They were going away for the following week—reluctantly. They were afraid to leave Mary alone, but she had school and couldn't go with them. Besides, she told them she was looking forward to the solitude, time to grieve alone. Her grief wasn't helped by having other people around. She seldom felt like talking about Jerry. She didn't know why she'd agreed to go to the party tonight, but she had. Savey had insisted, and Savey had a domineering personality. He had spent the entire past week persuading her to go because he was going to perform with his band at the party. Savey had been Jerry's best friend, and now he was in love with Mary.

Mary lit a cigarette as she dressed. She had picked up the habit an hour after Jerry's funeral. Her mother came in, waving away the smoke. Neither of her parents could stand cigarettes.

Her mother was in her mid-forties, petite and graying, with kind eyes and a nervous way of holding her hand to her mouth when something was bothering her, which was all the time now that her daughter had lost a boyfriend to a bullet in the brain.

"So you're up," her mother said. "I was just going to wake you."

"How long was I out?" Mary squeezed into a pair of jeans two sizes too small for her. "An hour?"

"It was more like two."

"It's strange how time flies when you're having fun." Mary took a deep drag and exhaled a cloud of smoke. Come to Marlboro Country. Her mother wrinkled her nose.

"Do you have to smoke in the house?"

Mary put the cigarette out in a plant she hadn't watered in a month. "No. I don't."

"That's OK," her mother said quickly. "The party tonight sounds like fun. Savey was telling me about it on the phone. He called while you were sleeping."

Mary coughed as she tried to button her pants. "Is he still picking me up?"

"Yes." Her mother glanced in the direction of the other room. "Your father and I will be gone by the time you get home. I've taped the number of the hotel where we'll be staying on the refrigerator." She added, "Call whenever you want."

"I'll be fine. Don't worry about me." Her pants finally buttoned, Mary searched for a top. She didn't care much about clothes since Jerry died. She didn't know what a psychologist would think of that.

Her mother watched her rummage through her closet. "We don't have to go."

"Don't be ridiculous. Have fun." Mary plucked out a tight black T-top that showed off her breasts. "It'll be nice to have the house all to myself, anyway."

Her mother forced a smile. "What will you do?"

"Probably smoke all the time."

Her mother lost her smile. "Mary."

Mary held up a hand. "Don't say anything. It's a joke. I'll be fine. Jerry's dead. But people do die. In fact, we all die. I'll die someday. But today, I'm fine. If you call me while you're away, I'll hang up. You have more important things to do than worry about me."

Her mother was silent before answering. "No, I don't," she said simply.

Her mother went to help her father load the car. Mary finished dressing and lit another cigarette, smoking it in the bathroom with the door closed. She brushed her teeth and flossed at the same time. It was an experience.

Savey arrived, and her parents fussed over him. Savey reminded them of Jerry, and Mary believed they could pretend Jerry wasn't really gone when Savey laughed and joked with them. Savey had a wicked sense of humor. He teased her mother about how sexy her new hairstyle was.

"It has that New York fashion model look," he said. "You need the clothes to go with it. You already have the figure. I swear, Mr. Weist, if you're not careful you're going to lose this woman to a gigolo while you're away."

Only Savey could get away with such remarks with her father, who just laughed and agreed that his wife did look twenty years younger. When Savey started to ask if they were bringing "protection" on their trip, Mary wisely grabbed Savey's arm and pulled him outside to his car.

"Have you no shame?" Mary asked when they were rolling off down the street.

"Your mother enjoys the attention," Savey said.

"The question is, does my father enjoy *you* giving it to her?"

Savey waved his hand. "Your dad's cool. He was laughing."

Mary sighed. "Dad is cool."

Savey glanced over. "What's the matter?"

"Nothing."

"You look good."

Mary half smiled. "I always look good." She glanced at him. "You look great."

Savey did, as a matter of fact, look damn fine. He was six foot, wiry, with a shock of dark brown hair that fit his budding rock star persona perfectly. He wore expensive clothes: silk shirts, leather pants and jackets. His cheekbones were prominent, framing his deep set gray eyes. His hands were large, but fine; he could play guitar as well as sing. He was always laughing and his smile was mesmerizing. A lot of people, even before Jerry died, thought Mary should be with Savey. They were both "Beautiful People."

And Mary was certainly beautiful, but not in a traditional homecoming princess way. She was ethereal; her attraction seemed to spring from another dimension. Her eyes were such a dark blue they appeared black. She had copper brown skin—inherited from neither of her parents. Her hair was the same color brown, unbelievably thick and wavy. Her body was virtually flawless. Some guy at school had snapped her picture and sent it to a New York modeling agency that wanted to see her immediately. But Jerry died a week after the invitation arrived, so she never answered.

Mary's beauty was part of her psyche; she carried it with her into every situation. But she never flaunted it, at least not intentionally. It was just that people automatically reacted to the power of her physical presence. She didn't merely turn heads but imaginations. She was a rare combination of an eighteen-year-old who could play twenty-five on the big screen, but still appear to be a high school senior. Her innocence was "devilishly seductive," as Savey put it.

He nodded at her compliment. "Tonight's going to be great. I'll dedicate every song to you."

"Pamela will love that. How long a set are you going to play?"

"Forty minutes max. Pamela's not paying us."

Mary lit a cigarette. "Not with money you mean."

Savey smiled. "She is awfully nasty to me these days." He paused. "Do you think I should do her?"

Mary blew smoke. "Not if you want to pass your next blood test."

"She's not that bad."

"She's worse."

Savey nodded. "You're probably right." He added, "Did you know Ken is going to be there?"

Ken was Jerry's younger brother. Mary had seen Ken almost every day when Jerry was alive. She saw him still at school, of course. But they hadn't really talked since Jerry died. Ken had worshipped his older brother. Mary studied the burning end of her cigarette and thought of the young man, two years her junior. He didn't know what happened that night. No one knew, no one except her.

"That's nice" was all she said.

"I think he wants to talk to you."

"All right." But then she shook her head. "What is there to talk about?"

Savey was concerned. "Are you all right, Mary?"

6

She coughed. "Yeah, I'm great. I feel good. It's nice to get out."

"Your parents say you sleep all the time."

"I'm a growing girl. I need my rest."

Savey hesitated. "It still hurts."

"Yeah." She swallowed thickly and added, "Life is dust."

"Why do you say that?"

She shrugged. "I don't know. The words just came to me."

But she knew they were true.

She remembered another time, not so long ago, that she and Jerry and Savey were driving in this very car down this exact street. Five short weeks ago. They were on their way to dinner, then to a movie. It wasn't unusual for them to move as a threesome. Jerry was talking excitedly about a sculpture he was working on. No one at school could paint or sculpt like Jerry. He was truly inspired. It was curious how his last piece of art seemed to foreshadow his death.

But perhaps the majority of all art did foreshadow death. Mary wondered if creativity was one of humanity's ways of dealing with the darkness that was destined to follow even the most brilliant life. Draw or mold an image of beauty before your limbs stopped moving. Before they ceased twitching. Maybe the beauty would outlast the decay.

Mary's thoughts were black indeed.

But she had watched Jerry die.

She had watched his arms and legs twitch for the final time.

She had been alone then. Yeah, then and now.

"We don't have to go to the party," Savey said uncertainly.

"We'll go." Mary looked out the window at the dark streets and puffed on her cigarette. She spoke in a weary voice, "I've been looking forward to it all week."

2

Pamela Poole's house was the largest and gaudiest in Seedmont, the small rural town in northwest Idaho they called home. Pamela's father was the mayor. He had bought the job. He owned and ran a lumber mill twenty miles north of town, in the foothills of the Rockies. Rumor had it that Mr. Poole had bought his wife as well, and that she was now available for rent. In other words, Pamela's mother got around. It must be in Pamela's genes. In Mary's unbiased and nonjudgmental opinion, Pamela Poole was a total slut.

But Mary liked her. Mary was always drawn to extremes in people. Just look at Savey. He was a live wire, and these days she hung out with him more than anyone. And good old Jerry. In his day he had been pretty out there, fashioning naked goddesses with radiant auras and no heads. She had initially posed for his last work, an earth princess kneeling before an invisible guillotine. But Jerry had found her nude body too powerful a distraction. They made love twelve times a week. Sometimes thirteen. Those were the days—and nights.

Pamela met them at the door and immediately started yelling at Savey. She had an incredible voice. She was head cheerleader and her voice had the power of persuasion. If the football team needed to score, she *told* it to. And the players usually did what she said. Of course, some people just thought of Pamela as loud. She had a large mouth, very sexy. She had large breasts as well. Pamela was a three-dimensional blond cutout, who drew a tan from the winter snow. There was always a party going on around her. For four years she had planned on being Seedmont High's homecoming queen. But come their senior year, Mary had stolen the honor. Pamela both respected and hated Mary for it.

Incredibly, Pamela had been Jerry's first boyfriend.

She wanted him back till the day he died.

But not after that.

"Where the hell have you been?" Pamela asked Savey. "The rest of your band got here an hour ago. The party's in full swing. Your boys need a sound check. The gang wants some music." Pamela paused to catch her breath. "Hi, Mary."

"Hello, Pamela," Mary said.

Savey shrugged. "The party's only started now that we're here. And do I have to remind you that we're not getting paid."

Pamela smiled and cocked her head to one side. "I said I'd be happy to reimburse you."

"I told you," Mary muttered under her breath.

Savey grinned and put a hand to his heart. "The night is young and filled with promise." His eyes strayed to Mary. "What more could I want?"

Pamela missed the turn of his eyes, but Mary didn't.

Savey wanted her. He wasn't being disrespectful to Jerry's memory—not in his mind at least, and probably not in hers. Still, she couldn't sleep with him. She could hardly sleep with herself.

"I haven't promised you anything yet," Pamela said, grabbing his arm. "Get up in front of the room. Knock them dead." Oh, darn, she must have thought. I said the *D* word in front of the grieving widow. Pamela immediately glanced over her shoulder at Mary. "Sorry."

Mary smiled and shrugged. "I'm just here to have a good time."

Like the rest of you. Oh well, that was a lie. Mary waded into the party, drifting and drinking. Even before Jerry died she'd had a thing about wine, but only good wine. Pamela knew of her weakness and brought her a special bottle from her daddy's cellar, where the old man was probably tied up for the night. Mary drank three glasses straight. By the time Savey finally joined his group she was sitting on a sofa in a corner by herself trying without success to light a cigarette she kept dropping. She wasn't merely drunk, she was *stoned*. The alcohol hadn't lightened her mood. She still felt weighed down, and it was hard for her to breathe. Still, she smiled as Savey dedicated the first song to her, the Police's "Don't Stand So Close to Me."

Savey's band was called Cool Covers. Savey had the voice and the licks, but had never written a decent song in his life. Without exception, the band played other people's material. Savey began to bump and grind. His band pounded behind him. Mary found herself laughing, hard; he was looking at her too much, gesturing obscenely. But then she had to turn her head away because her chuckles turned to tears. She was the saddest creature of all—an unhappy drunk. The band was loud. No one noticed.

Except perhaps Ken, Jerry's kid brother.

Suddenly Mary realized he was sitting beside her. Ken was not as handsome as Jerry. Jerry had been cut from marble. Ken was papier-mâché—a little droopy. He was not merely thin but malnourished, not that she was wolfing down the calories these days herself. When you went to hell and back, as the old saying went, you didn't pack a lunch. Ken wore large black-framed glasses, perched on top of his nose. He was only sixteen but already chronically slouched. Still, there was something endearing about his face. Wisps of blond hair fell over his forehead and eyes. He had a kind smile, a hesitant but sincere manner of speaking. Mary didn't know how long he had been staring at her but she offered him a drink. He shook his head.

"I'm my group's designated driver," he said.

"Oh." Mary blinked, and then held the bottle upside down. "I hope I'm not ours."

There was a break in the music. Savey was giving out his business card to all the females. Ken spoke uneasily. "It's good to see you, Mary," he said.

Mary dropped the bottle on the floor. Let Mrs. Poole pick it up, she thought. "It's seen to be good," she mumbled. "I mean, it's good to see you." She reached over and took his hand. "How are you? Really?"

He patted her hand and sank deeper into the couch. "Horrible."

"It doesn't get better, does it? I keep expecting it to, but that old thing about time is BS. It doesn't heal wounds." She burped. "It just makes them rot."

"Why did you come tonight?" Ken asked.

Mary withdrew her hand and put it on her belly. She wasn't sure, but she thought she'd throw up sometime in the next hour. "I heard you were going to be here."

Ken shook his head. "You've been avoiding me at school."

"That's true. Savey talked me into coming." She added, because she was not in her right mind, "He loves me, you know."

Ken nodded. "Jerry always knew that."

"I suppose you're right."

Ken hesitated. "Do you love him?"

"No." Mary sighed and briefly closed her eyes. "I love my pain. It's all I have. It's probably all you have. You have to love it, don't you?"

"Mary."

She waved her hand. "I'm babbling, I know. Why don't you get drunk with me? We can act silly. We can throw up on each other."

"Are you really drunk?"

"I don't know. I suppose."

"I need to talk to you."

She drew back and shook her head. "I can't talk about what happened. I'm sorry."

"I don't want to talk about that night. I just want to talk about my brother." Ken paused. "I feel like he's still here. Like he's watching us, waiting for something to happen so that he can contact us." Another pause. "Do you feel that way, Mary?"

The question was disturbing in the extreme.

For many reasons.

"No," she said softly.

Ken was not fooled. "You're lying. There must be a reason for my feeling."

Mary shook her head again. "We're both just screwed up, that's all." She searched for her lighter. "Where's my Bic?"

"It's in your hand."

"Oh." He was right. She reached for the pack of cigarettes, in her purse. The one she had dropped on the floor ten times looked kind of dirty. She didn't know why she smoked. It brought her no pleasure. Ken continued to stare at her.

"I think he's still here," he repeated.

"You have to stop thinking if that's what's going on in your head." She steadied a fresh cigarette in her mouth and flicked her Bic. "It's over, done, finished. It's tragic but it's not complicated." But her hand trembled as the flame blurred in her wasted vision. "We're not going to see him again."

Ken spoke with feeling. "I want to try to contact Jerry. I want a bunch of us to try."

Mary dropped her lighter and cigarette. The flame went out instantly. "What?" she whispered.

"I talked to Pamela. She said it would be all right."

Mary struggled to keep up. "What would be all right?"

"Tonight, after the party, we're going to have a seance. We're going to see if we can reach Jerry."

Mary was having trouble breathing. "Are you going to the cemetery?"

"No. We'll do it here. We'll let him come to us." Ken added, "Will you join us? Please? We need you, I'm sure, to make it work."

Mary's stomach rumbled, and a wave of dizziness swept over her. Still, she stood up. She had to get away from this kind of talk. It was too insane, and too real.

"Excuse me," she said, snatching up her coat. "I have to vomit."

3

Outside, in the wide backyard that stretched into the dark woods, she emptied her stomach into the bushes. Three times, in fact, choking on the burning bile that gushed up with the wine. But afterward she felt much better, relatively speaking. At least she no longer felt drunk. Her head was clear enough to regret whatever she had just said to Ken. Behind her, in the house, the noise of the party sounded revolting. She decided to take a walk in the woods, even in the cold night air. Maybe she'd freeze to death. Maybe a bear would attack her. Or perhaps a witch would find her, cast a spell on her, and steal her soul. The possibilities were endless and not without promise.

Mary lit a cigarette and walked into the trees. She started to think about Jerry. She thought about him all the time, of course, but now the memory was brighter, sober and red though it was. Jerry had gone to high school with her, but they hadn't really spoken until they stumbled upon each other in these very woods. Fourteen short months ago—it didn't seem possible. The primary reason she couldn't let go of the pain of Jerry's death was because, even when he was alive, she couldn't imagine living without him.

The day she met him had been enchanted. She had gone for a walk in the fall woods to search for inspiration for a short story she was writing for the school paper. The story was actually half done, but she was stuck at the part where the evil priests threw her heroine, an Egyptian goddess, into a tomb. Since the tale dealt with premature burial, she assumed it was a horror story. Especially since she couldn't figure out a way to liberate the young goddess from the tomb without getting ridiculous. She never did finish the story.

Jerry was painting when she ran into him. He had his easel, his brushes, his oils—all set up. Ironically, his subject matter had nothing to do with trees and the fall foliage. He was painting a skeleton crawling out of the sand behind a spaceship that had just landed on Earth. The door of the ship was open, and two vaguely insectoid creatures were descending a long silver plank to the ground, two beings whose precise physical details were obscured by long shadows. The thrust of the painting was that the skeleton was going to get the aliens; that it was the last of its kind, ready to live again, anxious to kill the aliens and steal their spaceship. Mary found the work disturbing and inspiring at the same time. She hadn't known Jerry could even draw; he took no art classes at school. She fell in love with the creation before the creator. Before the sun set that day, he was painting her.

Why did she love him? Because of his talent? His good looks? No, she thought, it was destiny. The woods that surrounded Seedmont were wide and deep. She could have walked in them twenty years, with Jerry doing the same, without stumbling on him. Particularly since she met him several miles from the nearest road. But it was destined that she'd meet him in that place far from everyone at school. Because it was only when they were alone that they could be complete with each other. He was the rose, she the thorn. She was the tree, he was the earth. She could not stand without him, not after she began to lean on him for support. Throughout their relationship, they often returned to the woods.

The first time they made love was in the trees.

As they had the last time.

Did he know it would be the last time?

"I feel like he's still here. Like he's watching us, waiting for something to happen so that he can contact us."

No, it felt like it had been the next to the last time.

What a thought to have.

Mary stopped and leaned against a tree, lighting another cigarette and letting the smoke sink into her lungs, into her blood, where it might poison her very soul. She pretended for a second that the tree was Jerry. But then the horror of its stiffness reminded her of his corpse. His beautiful blond body rotting in a hole in the ground. Really, they should have burned him and scattered his ashes in an unknown spot. They should have burned her as well. She wanted to die. She just didn't want to kill herself. And she didn't know how to ask a loved one to do it for her.

"Mary," a voice said.

Mary didn't even open her eyes. Voices in the nighttime woods didn't scare her. Even the voice of the devil couldn't, unless he told her that Jerry had gone to hell while she was destined for heaven.

"What?" she muttered.

Savey touched her back. "Are you all right?"

"Yes. I'm just molesting this tree."

He came around to her side. "Everyone's looking for you."

She shook her head and turned her back to the tree, still leaning against it. Finally she opened her eyes. "They are not looking for me."

The woods were very dark. Savey was a mere silhouette in his black jacket and pants, a line drawn on black paper. But that was the trouble with black papers, and tragic memories. You couldn't erase them. You could only tear up the whole thing and start over.

"I'm through singing," he said. "They're playing records now." He paused. "Do you want to dance?"

She gestured around them. "Yeah, out here. I want to make it with the fairies and gnomes and the dwarfs."

Savey shrugged. "Fine. Should I get us some more wine?"

"You smell it on me?" she asked.

"Actually, you smell like vomit."

"Thank you," she said.

He didn't know what to do with her. But he knew not to push her. That was one of the good things about Savey. He was desperate to make love to her, perhaps desperate in his own sick way to feel that a part of

Jerry survived through him. She believed she symbolized many wicked things for Savey. Because she did not think Savey's love for her was purely physical, or even completely natural. Not that she could talk. She leaned over and kissed him on the cheek.

"Do I really smell that bad?" she asked.

He considered, perhaps wondering if she was finally opening the door to him. "Just your breath."

She shivered. "How long have I been out here?"

"I saw you leave Pamela's an hour ago." He paused, taking a step back. She thought she heard a note of disappointment in his voice. "I saw you talking to Ken. Did he tell you what he wants to do?"

She chuckled softly. "He wants to have a seance. Isn't that ridiculous?"

"Yeah. Want to do it?"

She threw away her cigarette. Let Smokey the Bear worry about the burning embers. "What for?"

"Ken wants to—"

"I know what he wants to do," she interrupted sharply. Then she quieted and repeated herself. "It's ridiculous."

"Yeah."

She considered. She was already out on a limb. Did it really matter if she invited a family of gorillas to shake the branch for her? She was bound to fall anyway.

"How many are still there?" she asked.

"Dozens. But they'll start to leave soon."

She shook her head. "We're not going to contact Jerry."

Savey nodded and took her arm. "But we might contact something."

4

As Savey predicted, the party died a natural death. It got late and people grew tired. Most everyone considered Pamela's party a success, even if they didn't like her any more than they had before she invited them. For her part, Pamela seemed happy to say good night to so many people who had failed to vote her homecoming queen. She stood by the front door as they left and, when necessary, pointed them toward their cars. Feeling a headache coming on, Mary watched the exiting parade from a dark corner and thought that she would *never* invite any of these people to her house. Despite the fact that almost all of them had voted for her. She must have been in a bad mood. Thoughts of suicide could do that to you.

Who was left to summon the dead? Savey, Pamela, and Ken, of course, not to mention Mary herself. There were also the Chester twins. Radi and Tori Chester were identical genetic specimens. They were geniuses, together; their combined IQs added up to 150. Naturally, when either was alone, she or *she* was close to being a moron, with only an IQ of 75. At school, most of their teachers let them take tests together, and they always did better using their two heads. It was hard to flunk two such nice-looking creatures. Although neither could be described as beautiful, both Radi and Tori had wonderful red hair, green eyes, and soft freckled skin that glowed in the moonlight and peeled in the sun. Savey—according to Savey—had slept with both of them at the same time. Mary figured that if they couldn't invoke Jerry, they would at least attract the attention of a newly dead pervert.

Mary spoke alone with Pamela in her bedroom before the seance.

Mary heard Ken had brought a Ouija board.

"Why did you agree to do this?" Mary asked.

Pamela was changing into silk sweats, while drinking a can of beer. "It seemed important to Ken," she said. "I didn't have the heart to tell him no."

"You hurt his feelings more by indulging his insanity," Mary said.

Pamela set her beer down and checked her face in the mirror above her chest-of-drawers. Pamela's room was large and drafty, a showroom for the display of teddy bears and expensive CD equipment. There was a mirror on the ceiling above the bed. Mary hated to think of Jerry's seeing himself in it.

"I understand it's a sensitive issue," Pamela said. "You don't have to do it if you don't want to. No one's twisting your arm. You can leave now."

Mary played with her lighter. She was no longer drunk, just slightly hung over. "I can't," she said. "Savey's my ride."

"I'll call a cab for you."

"Do you want me out of here? You're not going to contact Jerry, you know. You're all just stroking yourselves."

Pamela turned to her. "You think I hate you. You're wrong. I'm sympathetic to you. I loved Jerry, too. Not as much as you, but enough to know how hard it must be for you to lose him."

Mary put away her lighter. "Well, I appreciate that."

"I mean it. I really do.

Mary held her eye. "I don't want your sympathy."

Pamela put her hands on her hips. "What do you want then?"

To stop breathing. To grow cold and lie perfectly still.

Mary's hard demeanor faltered. "I just want him back." She added with a wry smile, "I'm that stupid."

"You're anything but stupid." Pamela studied her for a few seconds. "Something else is bothering you."

Mary spoke with her head down. "I think we'll be making a big mistake to hold this seance."

"Why?"

"I don't know." Mary raised her head and wrapped her arms around herself as if she were cold. "I just think that Ken's going to get the opposite of what he wants."

Pamela snorted. "You're being silly. You were right the first time. We're just stroking ourselves."

"I hope so," Mary said.

5

The seance was held in the library. At the last minute Radi and Tori miraculously produced a crystal ball to sit beside the Ouija board. The sudden appearance of the ball made Mary realize that this seance had been planned long in advance. She questioned Savey about this, but he said he hadn't known anything about it.

Pamela had added esoteric touches to the library in honor of "their experiment," as she had begun to call what they were doing. There were the requisite candles and sticks of incense. Pamela had also brought down from her bedroom a foot high copper pyramid, which she said she had bought in a California New Age shop the previous summer. This she placed on a nearby stool, adjacent to the table, beside a cluster of candles. Glistening in the orange light, the copper reflected strange colors around the room.

Still, it was the crystal ball that bothered Mary, even more than the Ouija board, which was standard toy store fare. She couldn't imagine where the twins had found the crystal. The blasted thing rested in a silver holder in the shape of a dragon, and Mary didn't relish sitting so close to the demonic face of the creature. It seemed to stare at her with particular interest.

The library table was a small-size oak affair. They were all able to reach the Ouija board's planchette without having to leave their respective chairs. Mary ended up with a Chester twin on either side. While waiting for Pamela to finish lighting the candles, Radi and Tori spoke to Mary. As usual Mary was not positive who was who, and didn't much care. But it was probably Radi, on her right, who started the conversation. Radi usually wore more makeup than Tori, and applied it twice as badly.

"Are you excited?" Radi asked innocently.

Mary responded graciously, out of respect for the

small brain. "Yeah. I always love talking to my dead boyfriend."

Radi smiled. "You think he'll come?"

"Sure. Why not?"

Tori joined in. "How will we know if it's really Jerry?" she asked.

"He could spell out his name," Radi suggested.

Tori was not satisfied with such penetrating proof. "I hope he tells us something that only Jerry could know."

"If only Jerry knows it, then none of us will," Savey observed.

Tori flushed; she was so impressed. "God. That's right."

Mary wished she was still drunk.

"We'll know it's Jerry by the way he talks," Radi said.

"He's not going to talk," Tori said. "He's just going to spell out words."

"But Jerry never could spell that good," Radi said. "We'll know it's him if he messes up a few words."

"Jerry could never spell that *well*," Mary corrected.

"Huh?" both Radi and Tori said together.

"*Good* is the opposite of *bad*," Mary explained. "*Well* is the word you want." She paused and continued in an annoyed voice. "But what are you guys talking about anyway? Jerry spelled just fine."

"Does this Ouija board come with a spell check?" Savey asked Ken.

Radi was insulted. "We are not guys," she told Mary. "We are girls."

Mary got up. "Then you two *girls* should sit together, and mind meld, or whatever it is you need to do to stop talking like idiots. Just quit bothering me."

"She's in a *bad* mood," Radi told her sister.

"She's not *well,*" Tori said sympathetically as she moved to take Mary's spot.

Why was she putting herself through this, Mary asked herself for the tenth time. Pamela had finished creating the ambiance and was sitting down at the table with them now. A suicidal girlfriend, a depressed brother, a wannabe rock star, an oversexed cheerleader, and two brain-dead sisters—these were not going to penetrate the greatest mystery of all time. Especially not after a party of booze and loud music. If she had half a brain, she would call a cab or walk home.

Yet Mary stayed. She realized that even though the setting and the gang were outrageous, they were also, in their own warped states, perfect for what they were about to attempt. Because each of them was totally out there. Dancing on the perimeter so to speak. And they would have to go all the way out there to contact the dead. Yeah, Mary thought the whole thing was stupid, but there was a small part of her that was praying it might work. And there was a larger part of her that was terrified that it would.

She had her reasons. Boy, did she.

The lights were off. They had only candlelight.

Pamela picked up the Ouija board planchette, or the William Fuld message indicator—the proper name for the V-shaped plastic oracle pointer. Mary was surprised to see that the writing on it mentioned something about the U.S. patent office. Imagine that —Parker Brothers had patented the spirit world

Internet. Pamela studied the thing as if searching for flaws and then set it back down on the board.

"Now," Pamela began seriously, playing the role of the modern high priestess. "I have used this before, and it can blow your mind, or it can piss you off. If we screw around, the board screws with us. But if we're serious about what we're trying to do, we might get a serious response."

"What kind of responses have you gotten in the past?" Savey asked.

"They've been very interesting," Ken said.

Mary looked over at him. "So you've tried this before?"

"We did not try to contact Jerry before," Pamela said quickly.

"Not directly," Ken added.

Mary snorted softly. "You just put in a request for any recently dead relatives or friends? Any that happened to be in the astral neighborhood?"

"Like I said," Pamela responded stiffly, "if you have a bad attitude, it wrecks the whole thing." She paused. "But we don't want you to go, Mary."

"We need you, I'm sure, to make it work."

Mary spoke to both Ken and Pamela. "Did whatever you contacted before request that I be here? Is that what all this is about?"

Ken and Pamela exchanged looks. Now that they were getting close to actually doing it, Ken no longer seemed so confident. He looked scared, actually, as if he had just woken from a bad dream. But Pamela wore an elusive expression, one of her favorites.

"It did mention your name," Ken said softly.

"It?" Savey said. "Who was it?"

"We don't know," Pamela said. "We didn't get a name. It didn't want to give us one."

"That's cool," Radi said.

"What did it give you?" Savey asked.

Pamela held up a hand. "Look, let's just do it and see what comes through. Too much talking about this sort of thing is a waste of time."

"That's just what I was going to say," Tori said.

"How did it mention my name?" Mary insisted.

Pamela sighed and stared at the candles on the library mantle, strumming her fingers on the top of the oak table. Ken slouched back in his chair, pushed up his thick glasses, and looked worried.

"It just spelled it out," Ken said finally.

"No context?" Mary asked.

"No," Pamela said flatly and glanced at Ken, who had lowered his head.

"No," Ken said softly, agreeing.

"Cool," Radi said again.

"Oh shut up," Mary said. Brushing back her long hair, she reached for the planchette. "Let's get this over with."

"Just a second," Pamela said, lifting a pad of paper and a pen from the floor. "We need a scribe. Someone to write down what the planchette spells out."

There were no volunteers, except for Radi, who didn't count because she couldn't spell, even when the letters were read to her one by one. In the end Pamela was forced to keep track of what was printed out. She didn't seem to mind, too much. The rest of them lightly placed their fingertips on the planchette.

"Just close your eyes and relax," Pamela whispered.

"If we close our eyes we won't be able to see," Tori said wisely.

"Just for a few minutes, until it starts moving," Pamela said softly, leaning toward the board, her expression eager. Obviously, she wasn't about to take her own advice about not watching.

Mary closed her eyes and sat for a minute or two, feeling rather stupid. Because the planchette just lay beneath their fingers, doing nothing. Beside her, she heard Savey fidget, and wondered if he felt as she did.

Yet, a minute after that, ever so slightly, the planchette began to move. It did nothing special, really, just described tiny circles.

"Who's doing this?" Radi asked. "Is it you, Tori?"

"No," Tori said. "I think it's moving by itself."

"It is," Pamela said. "Open your eyes, all of you, and relax. Let it do what it wants to do for a few minutes before asking it any questions."

What it wanted to do, Mary soon saw, was to move around in larger and larger circles. Soon it was going pretty fast, dancing just beyond the letters, and it was hard to believe that someone in the group was not moving it consciously. But glancing around, Mary was convinced no one was purposely manipulating the thing. Everyone looked, well, too intrigued. Even Ken; his fear seemed to have changed to expectation.

Finally, the planchette slowed to a crawl.

And then pointed at *Yes.*

"Yes," Radi said. "What does that mean?"

"I don't know," Tori replied. "The opposite of no maybe."

"It's asking what we want to ask," Pamela said, her

face flushed. In the dark light of the candles, she looked something like a witch. It was clear to Mary that Pamela already had a series of questions figured out to ask it. Pamela spoke directly to the board, ignoring the rest of them.

"Is someone there?" Pamela asked.

It moved away from the *Yes*, then returned sharply.

"Wow," Radi said. "It can hear us."

"Shh," Pamela said. "It's better to have one person talk. Otherwise, you confuse the energies." She paused. "Who's there?"

The planchette began to jump to the letters, quickly.

S . . . O . . . M . . . E . . . O . . . N . . . E

"Someone," Pamela muttered, as she finished writing down the word. "Does this someone have a name?"

The planchette swung between *Yes* and *No*.

"Could you be more specific?" Pamela asked.

No.

"Where are you?" Pamela asked, still taking notes.

Here.

"You are here with us?"

Yes.

"Do you want to be with us?"

Yes. No. Yes. No.

"Why then do you come here to be with us? If you are not sure you want to be here?"

I am drawn.

"Oh Jesus," Radi said, scared.

"Shh. Does one of us draw you?" Pamela asked.

Yes.

"Just one of us?" Pamela asked.

Yes.

"Which one of us draws you here?"

It hesitated.

Mystery.

"Do you know who draws you here?" Pamela persisted.

Yes.

"Would you rather not tell us?"

Yes.

"Because it could upset this person?"

Yes.

"Do you care about this person?"

Yes.

"It is your care for this person that draws you here?"

Yes.

"Do you care about the rest of us?"

Yes.

"Do you experience love?"

Yes.

"Do you love us all?"

Yes.

"But you love one of us more than the rest of us?"

Yes.

"Are you human?"

No.

"Are you dead?"

No death.

"You are alive?"

There is no death.

Pamela considered. "Interesting. But by our standards, are you dead?"

It hesitated.

No.

"Were you ever human?"

It hesitated.

Short time.

"How long ago were you human?"

Long time ago.

"Did you live in a particular country that we know of?"

Yes.

"What country was that?"

Egypt.

"You were alive in ancient Egypt?"

It hesitated.

Yes.

"Why do hesitate?" Pamela persisted.

Mystery.

"Can you explain this mystery to us?"

Difficult.

"Do you wish you were human now?"

Yes. No. Yes. No.

"What are you now?"

Mystery.

"Are you a ghost?"

No.

"Are you an angel?"

Mystery.

"Are you a devil?"

No.

"Are there devils?"

It hesitated.

Yes.

"Have you ever seen a devil?"

It hesitated.

Yes.

"Did the devil scare you?"

It hesitated.

Mystery.

"Can you experience fear?"

It hesitated.

For you.

"You can be afraid for us?"

Yes.

"Are you afraid now for us?"

It hesitated. A long time.

Yes.

"Oh God," Radi whispered, trembling.

"Shh," Pamela said, focused on the board still. "There's nothing to be afraid of."

It was not a question. Whoever was listening did not have to answer. But it did.

Are you sure?

Mary almost took her hands off the planchette at the last response. Indeed, she practically stood and left the room. But not for the obvious reason of the disturbing nature of the reply—to a question that hadn't even been asked. Her disquiet had a more subtle origin. For her, the room had suddenly chilled. Yet, with the last response, she felt a strange warm current touch the base of her spine. It was not electrical; it wasn't exactly physical. Nor was it caused by an emotional response. She was sure of that. Yet she nevertheless felt it with her nerves. And she knew that no one else in the room had felt it.

The entity was talking about her. She had drawn it.

Pamela was staring at her.

"Is it all right if I ask about Jerry?" she asked.

Mary smiled faintly, miserably. "Do whatever you want."

"No," Radi said suddenly. "We shouldn't do that."

"Shut up," her sister told her.

Pamela turned her attention back to the board.

"Do you know Jerry Rickman?" Pamela asked.

It hesitated.

Yes.

"Are you Jerry Rickman?"

The room held its breath. But the answer came swift.

No.

"Are you connected to Jerry?"

All connected.

"But are you here because of Jerry's death?"

It hesitated.

Indirectly.

"Do you know where Jerry is?"

Yes.

"Can you contact him?"

It hesitated.

Mystery.

"Do you want to contact him?"

No.

"Would you allow us to contact him?"

No.

"Is Jerry all right? Where he is, I mean."

It hesitated.

For now.

"Can something harm him?"

Mystery.

Pamela grew impatient. "No. Don't say that. Explain. How can a dead person be harmed?"

No death.

"Then he can't be harmed?"

Mystery.

Pamela tried another tack. "Is the theory of reincarnation genuine?"

Yes. No. Yes. No.

"Are people born many times? Do they evolve through many lives?"

Yes. Yes.

"Then there is reincarnation?"

Not as you understand.

"Will Jerry be reborn?"

It hesitated.

Hopefully.

"Is there something that can stop him from being reborn?"

Yes.

"Is that a bad thing?"

It hesitated.

A nightmare.

Pamela was intent. "Can the person who draws you here be the cause of Jerry's failure to be reborn?"

Yes.

"What will—what can this person do to stop his rebirth?"

It hesitated.

Nightmare.

"Could you please specify what form this nightmare might take?"

The planchette got excited.

No. No. No. No.

"I don't like this," Radi whispered.

"Is this nightmare imminent?" Pamela asked.

It hesitated.

Don't know.

"Does your coming help prevent this nightmare?"

No.

"Does it help cause it to occur?"

It hesitated.

Maybe.

"Then why do you come?"

I am drawn.

"You are drawn despite the danger?"

Yes.

Pamela considered. They all did.

"Are you drawn here to this person because of something that happened in the past?"

Yes.

"Was it long ago in the past?"

Yes.

"Was it when you were in ancient Egypt?"

Yes.

"Did something happen then that draws you back now?"

Yes.

"Was Jerry alive then?"

Yes.

"Were any of us alive then? When you and Jerry were alive?"

Yes.

"Was I?" Mary blurted out, not meaning to.

It hesitated.

Yes. No.

Pamela was confused. "She was either alive or she wasn't alive."

34

The Ouija board was silent.

"Was Mary in incarnation at that time?" Pamela rephrased the question.

Yes. No.

"Was I a human being?" Mary asked, once again not wanting to. But something compelled her—perhaps the charge at the base of her spine, which had slowly, softly, begun to move toward her head. The Ouija board gave its longest answer yet.

You thought you were a god.

"That's funny," Radi said and chuckled. "Mary wanted to be an Egyptian god."

"Shh," Pamela said. "What happened in ancient Egypt that draws you back now?"

It hesitated.

Nightmare.

"And there is a possibility this nightmare might reoccur now?"

Worse.

"In ancient Egypt, did the nightmare involve Jerry?"

Yes.

"Now, today or in the near future, could it involve Jerry again?"

Yes.

"Could it involve Mary?"

Yes.

"Is Mary the source of the problem?" Pamela asked.

Savey interrupted. "Pamela. Let's not get personal."

Pamela hushed him. "Shh."

But the Ouija board did not respond.

"Does Mary still think she is a god?" Pamela asked.

It hesitated.

None know her.

"But do you know her?" Pamela insisted, and there was a ruthless note in her voice. The board was not offended.

Yes.

"Do you know what she did in the past?"

Yes.

"Was it evil?"

It hesitated.

Unnatural.

"Her desire to be a god was unnatural?"

It hesitated.

Many things were in those days.

"What about in these days?"

Mystery.

"Do you know what happened the night Jerry died?"

Yes.

"Were you there?"

It hesitated.

Yes.

Pamela glanced at Mary and licked her lips. Mary knew what the next question would be, and the one after that. Really, it was now obvious what Pamela had been leading up to. Pamela had had no intention of letting Mary leave that night. Not before the seance. Maybe not after it, if she got the information she was seeking. But that was all right, Mary thought. She just gave Pamela a cold stare and nodded slightly. It didn't matter—nothing did. It was just a goddamn Ouija board talking. It couldn't be used in a court of law.

"Was Mary there the night Jerry died?" Pamela asked finally.

"Pamela," Savey complained. "Now you're being insensitive."

Mary noticed Ken leaning forward. To see the answer.

Ask her.

"We have asked her," Pamela insisted. "She says she was not there."

The Ouija board did not respond.

"Is Mary lying?" Pamela asked.

"This is heavy," Radi said.

You lie. She lies. All lie.

Pamela was annoyed. "It was a nightmare the night Jerry died. We just want to put that nightmare behind us. Can't you answer our questions?"

It did not hesitate.

The nightmare is before you.

Savey took his fingers off the planchette. "I want to stop this. I should never have consented to it. I didn't know this was going to be a Mary-bashing session. Ken, did you plan this with Pamela?"

"We didn't plan anything," Pamela interrupted. "We just want to know what happened that night." She turned to Mary. "I've read the police report. So has Ken. We got the feeling there are a few holes in it. Like where were you when the bullet entered Jerry's brain."

Mary ignored Pamela and turned to Ken, who sat hunched over, staring at the planchette as if it would somehow save him from memories none of them could forget. Mary didn't feel angry then, just overwhelmingly sad.

"Do you have questions for me?" she asked him.

Ken shook his head faintly. The questions had worn him down. He was clearly exhausted. "No, Mary," he said quietly.

"Damnit!" Pamela said. "You want to know as much as I do. We have a right to know."

Mary spoke calmly. "What gives you the right, Pamela? You're not a god. You're not even homecoming queen."

Pamela held her eye a long time. "Yeah, that's right. That makes sense. He died just before you were nominated."

"I don't get this," Radi said to her sister.

"I'll explain it to you later," Tori said confidently.

Mary gestured to the Ouija board. "I have nothing to hide. If I've drawn this entity or angel or god here, he has my permission to answer all your questions." She paused and leaned closer to Pamela. She spoke in a slightly mocking tone. "You can even ask it if I pulled the trigger. I don't mind."

Pamela continued to study her. "Two people died that night. Did you kill them both?"

Mary very slowly smiled. "You don't want to ask the oracle?"

"Not when I can ask the god," Pamela said.

Mary glanced at Ken. "What do you think?" she asked.

Ken spoke to Pamela, his voice heavy with reluctance. "The evidence clearly shows that the security guard shot my brother." He turned to Mary. "But I do wonder who shot the guard."

Savey grabbed Mary's hand to pull her to her feet. "You guys are sick. We're getting out of here."

Mary did consent to stand, as a prelude to leaving. But she continued to stare at all of them. And it would have been an understatement to say they continued to stare at her. Yet this moment that she had dreaded above all others gave her a strange sense of power. The subtle current in her spine had reached her brain and she was full of unnatural energy, perhaps even of the black kind. Yes, truly, she felt like a god right then. She chuckled at their accusations, but a tear somehow managed to run over her cheek.

"I loved Jerry," she said. "You don't kill what you love."

"Not on purpose," Pamela whispered.

Savey tried to grab Mary's hand again, but she held him off. Mary suddenly leaned over and kissed Pamela on the cheek, catching her by surprise. She whispered in her ear.

"Thanks for the party and the seance." She drew back and patted Pamela on the head as if she were a servant. "Good night, and sweet dreams."

Savey and Mary left then.

Just left the Ouija board lying on the table.

And the entity—it did not get to finish.

6

Mary and Savey did not talk on the ride home. Savey tried to, naturally, but Mary ensured the silence by staring out the window, away from him. But when they reached her house and he asked if he could come in, she said sure.

Inside, since she wouldn't talk to him, he tried to kiss her. She didn't encourage the intimacy, but she didn't push him away either. As a result she ended up pinned against the door that led to the family room while he moved his lips all over her face. He had very sensual lips. The faint smell of alcohol on his breath was also nice. But he was not Jerry. He could never be Jerry. He stopped a minute into the seduction.

"It's too soon?" he asked.

She focused on the floor. "It's too late."

He spoke with feeling. "But maybe if we hold each other, we can comfort each other." He took her by the shoulders. "I love you, Mary. Do you know that?"

She nodded weakly. "I do."

"Then make love to me. Let me spend the night."

"No."

"Why do you say no?"

"I don't know."

He paused. "You need me."

She sighed, still gazing down. "I need something."

He pulled her into his arms. "I need to touch you. It's a physical necessity. I just can't let it go. I can't let you go."

She looked at him then, smiled at him, brushing his wild hair from his sad gray eyes. He was begging to have sex with her and yet seemed to be on the verge of tears. None of this was natural. None of this was meant to be. She couldn't say no to him, and she could not say yes.

"Build a fire," she said finally. "Give me a massage. I'll take off my clothes."

He hesitated. "Should I take off my clothes?"

She shook her head. "Not tonight."

While Savey started the fire, Mary took a long shower, another ritual of hers these days. It wasn't unusual for her to spend an hour each day in the shower, with the water almost hot enough to burn her. There was dirt on her aura that she had to wash away. But water wasn't strong enough. She needed an exorcism.

When she returned to the family room, she was surprised at the size of the fire Savey had constructed. It was a funeral pyre. Why, she could just lie on it and let the flames lick her flesh, instead of his tongue. A howling wind that promised snow had come up outside, not unusual for late November. It rattled the back door, or else it was the Grim Reaper knocking. Let me in. We have somewhere to go, not far from here. But we will not be coming back. . . . Oh, if the black knight would only come. She would welcome him.

The nightmare is before you.

Mary wore only a towel. As she lay down, it still covered her butt. But Savey had found some scented oil, and as he began to work it into her back, the towel slipped to the side and she lay exposed. She didn't care. She liked having her butt rubbed, and other things. Still, she would not have intercourse. She feared if she did a portion of the poison in her soul would enter Savey's, and he would know no comfort at all. She really did care about him, maybe love him. Her naked body seemed to take his breath away.

"You're very beautiful," he whispered, rubbing her thighs.

"Thank you," she muttered, her face resting on her folded arms.

"Does this feel good?"

"Yes."

"Should I do it harder?"

"I don't care."

He paused. "What do you care about these days?"

"Nothing."

"Even me? Am I a part of that nothing?"

She reached around and patted his knee. "No. You're something."

He leaned down and kissed the back of her neck. "I would love to lie down beside you."

She took her hand back. "Just rub me, OK?"

He returned to massaging her lower back. "You have incredible skin. It's copper colored, like your hair." He paused. "Do you know what it reminds me of?"

"What?"

"An Egyptian goddess."

She didn't smile. "What did you think of the dire statements on the Ouija board?"

"Not much. I was more concerned about Pamela's

attitude toward them, and toward you. You know what she was implying."

Mary spoke calmly. "She wasn't implying anything. She said it outright. She thinks I killed Jerry."

"That's so weird. I don't know why you didn't scream at her."

"I was not in a screaming mood."

"But she's infected Ken with her ideas."

"I don't know. Ken has his own mind."

"But why bring in something like an Ouija board to try to implicate you in Jerry's death? Why the sham of a seance?"

Mary turned her head so that she was looking at the fire. The flames warmed the right side of her body, yet she had gooseflesh on her left side.

"I think you're looking at it backward," she said dreamily, almost hypnotized by the fire. "I think they originally got their idea from the being who spoke through the board."

"You think there really was something there?"

"Yes."

Savey snorted. "That's ridiculous."

"The universe is ridiculous."

"It was only our subconscious moving the indicator."

"I felt something else there."

"What?"

"I can't describe it. There was a power. It touched me."

He leaned close again and spoke in her ear. "I want to touch you."

She continued to stare at the fire. "You are, Savey. Don't push it."

He caressed her bottom. "Tell me more about what you felt?"

"I can't. But whatever was there—it knew me."

"It was implying that you were evil. At least thousands of years ago."

"That didn't bother me. I probably was." She paused. "Did you know the day I met Jerry in the forest, I was writing a story about an Egyptian goddess?"

"No. Did you show the story to anyone?"

"No," Mary said. "I got stuck and never finished it. But what the Ouija board said—it reminded me of that story. Don't you find that interesting?"

"I still don't believe we were talking to anybody."

"Pamela does. And Ken."

"Why is Pamela trying to reopen this wound?" Savey said. "Can't she just let it be. She never cared that much about Jerry."

"Oh, you're so wrong. I think we saw tonight that she was still obsessed with Jerry when he died." She hesitated. "Maybe he was still seeing her."

"No way. I was his best friend. He would have told me if he was still interested in Pamela. Jerry's love for you was absolute."

Mary smiled sadly. "Did you two often talk about me?"

"All the time."

"Did you tell him that you were dying to get in my pants?"

Savey was long answering. "No. I never told him that." He paused. "Did you know?"

"Of course."

"You didn't mind?"

She gestured behind her. "I don't have my pants on now."

He put his palms on her shoulders. "Mary?"

"Yes?"

"I don't want to push."

"Then don't."

"Please, could you turn over. I need to kiss you."

"No. If I turn over, we'll make love. And I can't do that."

"Why not?"

She spoke to the flames. "Because I have no love. We'll make nothing, and we'll end up feeling worse than before."

7

After Savey had gone home, unsatisfied and confused, Mary donned a heavy woolen robe and climbed in her car and drove off. There was only one cemetery in Seedmont—Memorial Meadows. It was located so far into the woods that it was left largely unguarded. Not that they'd ever had trouble with grave robbers. At least, not until the cemetery had Jerry, and the darkness had her.

Mary parked behind the cemetery, on a stretch of unpaved road. The rear of the cemetery was a wall of pines—nothing else. The openness was inviting—for the disturbed. Anyone could just walk into the place and lie down on any grave. Mary climbed out of her car and stumbled in the dark toward Jerry's plot. There was no moon; she had no flashlight. But her feet knew the way to his body.

With her hands, Mary found his marker. With her fingers she traced his name and dates, etched in the granite like scratches on her soul. He had been buried only a month ago; his plot was naked earth. She was still naked beneath her robe. Yet, even in the freezing night air, even in the hard dirt, she lay down on top of the plot. She had done this before, many times, lying on top of her dead boyfriend, with six feet of dirt between them. It did nothing to soothe her pain. It just made her dirty, cold, and sick with perversion.

Still, she liked it. In a strange way.

It felt—familiar.

She remembered the night Jerry died.

It had been a Thursday night, two days before the big homecoming game and the crowning of the new queen. Indian summer had made a last rare appearance. The temperature, even after the sun went down, was in the high sixties. It was to be the last warm night of the year.

Jerry picked her up in his van. He needed a vehicle with space to spare because he was always off painting. They went for pizza and then for a walk in the woods. They ended up skinny dipping in a lake not far from the cemetery. Perhaps that was an omen. They made love in the trees and Mary got several needles stuck in her ass. But it was fun having Jerry pull them out.

Then Mary had the thought that killed Jerry.

She said, "I wonder if I was voted queen today."

And he said, "Why don't we break into the office and count the votes?"

She smiled at the wickedness of an idea that came to her then. "How do we know they haven't already been counted?"

He saw where her question was leading. "We don't know. But we're not going to alter the ballots, are we?"

Her smile grew. "It depends on how many have my name on them."

He was surprised. "You don't care about being queen, do you?"

She just laughed. "Of course not. It's all BS."

But she did care actually.

Mary, Queen of Seedmont—had kind of a ring to it.

Which thought killed Jerry? Maybe it was the last one. To be queen. To be important, like some kind of adolescent goddess. She worried that Pamela Poole would win. Pamela was also on the court, and she was pretty, Jerry's ex in fact. Plus she had slept with half the voting population of the senior class. Maybe if Pamela did win, Jerry would be impressed with her. Stranger things had happened.

"I want to see those ballots," she told him.

"Seriously?"

She kissed him on the mouth. "Do it for me."

They drove to the school. It was close to midnight. They never knew Seedmont High had security. Certainly they never imagined that a guard, if one existed, would be carrying a real gun with real bullets in it. They never intended any harm. They didn't even break the window they used to climb into the main office. Jerry just popped the latch with a bent wire hanger. But they didn't turn on the light when they were inside. They weren't stupid.

They found the ballots in a manila envelope on the principal's desk. It was a large envelope and it was stuffed. Jerry dumped the papers out in a pile on the floor and they dug into them with secret agent zeal. A shaft of light poured in from a hallway bulb. So many had cast their votes in pencil—and there was an eraser on the desktop. . . . If the count didn't go well, Mary decided, maybe she would tamper with destiny. Just a little. Jerry would never tell.

Yet quickly Mary saw that she had been voted homecoming queen by a landslide. They didn't need more than a quarter of the votes to see that over two-thirds of the student body loved her, and that only ten percent had thought Pamela was decent in bed. Mary couldn't believe she was so well thought of. She was basking in the glow of the confirmation when the light snapped on overhead and they saw the pale guard with the sweaty hand and the semiautomatic pistol.

"Put your hands over your heads," he gasped. "Slowly get to your feet."

Mary snorted. "Put down that gun. We go to school here."

The guard—he couldn't have been more than twenty—fingered the pistol's trigger. His eyes were liquid saucers. It was as if he had stumbled across an alien disemboweling the homecoming queen instead of two nice innocent kids. He was so scared, Mary wasn't even sure he was breathing.

"You just do what I say," the guard whispered.

"Do what he says," Jerry said softly to her, his hands already up.

Mary threw down her ballots and climbed to her feet, as fast as she wanted. She refused to put her arms in the air. As the guard took a step closer, she nodded toward his pistol.

"Better put that thing away," she said. "It doesn't look like you know how to use it."

The guard shook the weapon at her. "Put up your hands."

"No," she said.

"Mary," Jerry hissed, standing beside her, his fingers almost touching the ceiling.

"Put up your hands," the guard repeated.

Mary sneered. "Make me, tough guy."

The guard did something totally unexpected then. He seemed to be so frightened that Mary couldn't believe he'd move any closer. But perhaps his father —or even his mother—had taunted him as a child by calling him tough guy, when in fact he was a total wimp who needed to carry a gun to protect his milk money. Whatever the reason, he stepped forward and poked Mary hard in the belly with the barrel of his pistol. She doubled over in pain.

Unfortunately, the guard had just pushed Jerry's one button.

No one fooled with his Mary.

"Hey," Jerry swore and stepped forward to push the guard aside. But he never got that far. The guard turned and shot him in the right arm. He only nicked him, actually, but the sound of the detonating bullet and the sight of Jerry's blood shocked them all. Only later was Mary to question whether the guard intended to shoot Jerry at all. The guy was so nervous, and semiautomatic pistol triggers so notoriously sensitive. But at that moment all she saw was red. The blood seemed to gush from the outside of Jerry's right bicep as if from a crack in the dam of a reservoir of cherry-flavored soda. Jerry stared down at his wound as if he had just noticed a spider on his arm. The guard, also, seemed transfixed by the sight of the red stuff. He stood there dumb, his pistol still pointing at Jerry.

Mary went nuts, totally.

She jumped the guard. Just flew right at him.

They landed in a dangerous pile and the gun went off again. There was an explosion of glass and light, and they were plunged into darkness. She had never cared for the office's fluorescent strips. They rolled on the floor and she ended up on top of him, scratching his eyes, his mouth, his nose. Then she felt him trying to bring up the hand that held the gun. Immediately she grabbed the arm with both hands and leaned over and bit his wrist. The guard screamed in pain.

The gun went off again.

They were on the floor, the gun was pointed up at an angle.

Mary felt something heavy fall across the back of her legs.

Instantly she knew Jerry was dead.

"Let me go!" the guard screamed in terror.

What was he complaining about? He had just shot her boyfriend. That didn't make him a murderer, of course, because it was an accident. Nor was she a murderer then when she very carefully and very methodically began to bend his wrist so that the barrel of his pistol was now pointed at the side of his own head. He had his finger on the trigger. She never pulled it. In fact, she never touched it. But she kept struggling with him, screeching in his ears, with the complete and certain knowledge that the gun was eventually going off again. And when a fourth and final bullet was fired, and the guard went limp in her arms, she wasn't surprised.

Nor would she be guilty of anything in a court of law.

Calmly, Mary stood and took a deep breath.

The room had another light, which she turned on.

The guard had taken a bullet in the right temple. He lay grotesquely silent, staring at the ceiling with absolutely fixed eyes. He was not moving, and he was hardly bleeding. Jerry, on the other hand, was twitching like the Tin Man in an electrical storm. The blood that flowed from the center of his forehead was a torrential red river. It spread over the floor toward the piled ballots, a dark swell possessed of the evil desire to drown out her golden moment of glory. As it touched the first ballot, and the stain spread over the X that had been marked beside her name, Mary let out a pitiful moan.

"Jerry," she whispered, kneeling beside him, putting her hand over his wound. Incredibly his eyes were open; he was still alive. He stared at her with something akin to surprise. It was as if he didn't know he was hurt. Even though his limbs continued to kick spasmodically.

"Mary," he said quietly. "Are you all right?"

She wept. "Yes. I'm fine."

"Good." He briefly closed his eyes and drew in a shuddering breath. When he opened them again, however, he saw the blood on the floor, how it spread away from his head. Realization dimmed his expression. It couldn't be the easiest thing in the world to see that you'd just been shot in the head. He spoke with difficulty. "I don't feel so good, Mary."

She clasped his right hand, getting his blood all over it. "You've been hurt, that's why. You've just got to relax. I'll call the hospital, get you an ambulance." She froze. "Jerry? Jerry!"

His eyes were sinking back in his head. Not only that—it was as if his whole expression was being sucked up into the weird space where people went when they died. His lips puckered inward, the flesh on his cheeks wrinkled. Suddenly her eighteen-year-old boyfriend was a mummy, a prune, staring at her with ancient bloodshot eyes. He looked so sick right then, it broke her heart. But the voice that came out of him chilled her to the bone, the words he said. The raspy tone was coarse sandpaper scratched over a dry tombstone.

"Clareesh," he whispered. "The akasha burns. The sacrifice begins."

He seemed to grin. Without teeth.

Then he closed his eyes. His face returned to normal, except for the bloody hole in his forehead. And he died—her Jerry died. He just stopped breathing and sank back on the floor and left her. Left her with nothing.

"No," she said. "No."

But the facts said yes.

Mary stood and turned off the light.

She walked home. Her parents were out late. Her bloody clothes she burned in the fireplace, flushing the ashes down the toilet. Jerry was dead and there was nothing she could do. At the moment. She didn't want to complicate her life. That was the simplest reason she could think of to explain why she did what she did.

But simple truths are often white lies.

She took a long steamy shower that night, and was in bed asleep before her mom and dad returned. No one even knew about the deaths until the next morning, Friday. By then, of course, history had rewritten itself. She had said good night to Jerry at eleven, her report to the police said, and that was the last she saw of him.

They counted the ballots, even the bloody ones.

Saturday night, she was crowned homecoming queen, in absentia.

That Saturday night, she bought her first pack of cigarettes.

She smoked it, all of it, alone beside the plot where Jerry was to be buried.

9

Now, this night, the night of Pamela's party and the mysterious seance, Mary lay writhing on the ground above Jerry's well-buried corpse. Six feet of hard earth between them, she thought. That was a lot, it was the law. It was as if those damn undertakers didn't trust the nation of bereaved sweethearts. Didn't believe those left behind would willingly consent to keep their hands off the freshly dead.

Well, maybe they were right. Maybe one night soon she would bring a shovel to this place and dig. She hadn't gone to Jerry's funeral. She hadn't given him a proper goodbye. He deserved that at least, to feel her fingers on his lips one last time, her tongue on his brow. She wanted to touch him, she needed to. As Savey might have said.

It was her right.

Let the nightmare come. Who gave a damn.

Oh, but she knew it was sick. That she needed help.

Around three in the morning, Mary finally stood and walked toward her car. On the way she passed the guard's grave site. She'd heard he had a young wife, an infant child. But he had killed her Jerry, and that she could never forgive. She paused long enough to spit on the man's grave.

"Rest in peace," she said.

10

That night, while asleep in bed, Mary sensed a light. Even though she was unconscious, she seemed to know that it descended from on high. A white sun slowly falling into oblivion. For how long she experienced this approaching light, she didn't know. But it seemed as if she dreamed about it for thousands of years across a wide desert that shifted and moved. Ancient pyramids rose and crumbled. A sharp wind blew and the dry dust dispersed. The strange thing was—amidst the many other strange things in her life lately—she didn't know if she welcomed this light.

Even though she knew precisely from which part of the sky it originated.

But then she awoke. And knew nothing.

Except that her heart was pounding.

Why? She asked herself this as she sat up.

There was a white glow outside her window.

Mary stood and reached for a robe. Not the same one she had worn to the cemetery. That one was filthy with mud. This robe was a gift from Savey the previous Christmas. It was, consequently, too short and skimpy for practical use. It couldn't keep her warm on such a bleak wintry night. She shivered as she stepped to the window and looked out.

There was a flying saucer in the sky.

A big fat white one.

"Oh shit," she whispered.

The ship hovered perhaps three hundred feet above her house. It was at least a football field across, a brilliant circular disc with an array of tiny colored lights located along a perimeter that throbbed as she watched. Indeed, it was almost as if the lights were aware of and sensitive to her attention. As she followed their psychedelic patterns, they increased in intensity and complexity. It was as if she were observing a colored alphabet spelling out a cosmic language.

In utter silence. Not a sound came from overhead.

Mary's house was located at the edge of town,

slightly removed from other houses. Yet it wasn't entirely isolated. The glow from the flying saucer bathed in light a few other houses that she could see from her window. Mary thought the craft would be visible all over Seedmont. Any second now, she expected a dozen people to come running out of their houses screaming.

But that didn't happen.

So Mary decided to go outside. Herself.

To see if they wanted to take her away to an alien world.

Standing in her backyard, glowing like a silver sparkler beneath the mammoth firework, she reached up. Her hands spontaneously clasped together, the gesture almost prayerful. And perhaps there was a minor deity aboard the craft who heard her prayer. For suddenly the light tripled in brilliance, and she was forced to close her eyes and swear.

11

Then she was lying on Jerry's grave once more, and there was no flying saucer in the sky. There were plenty of stars, though. She had fallen asleep on top of his dead body. Not the first time. Feeling cold and sick, Mary stood and brushed herself off. It was only then she realized she was wearing the robe Savey had given her. Not the woolen one but the nasty one.

Mary's head jerked up once more.

Where was it. Why was it. Was it?

"Just a dream," she whispered to herself.

She walked toward her car, pausing only to spit on the guard's grave. But instead of her Toyota she found Jerry's van. The keys were in the ignition. She climbed inside and checked to see if there was gas in the tank. Actually, the tank was chock-full. Somebody could have fueled it up just outside the cemetery.

Mary drove it back to Jerry's house and parked out front.

She walked home in her skimpy robe.

She saw no one. And no one saw her.

At home, she went straight to bed.

12

Then she woke up again, and there was a white glow outside her window. Sitting up in bed, she listened as her heart pounded. She was naked. On the chair beside her bed were two dirty robes, both stained with mud.

"This is no dream," she whispered.

But was she scared? This young broken thing that just wanted to die? Yeah, she realized, she was terrified. She didn't want to go to the window but was compelled to do it. The colors called in the dark, the mysterious alphabet sang in silence. Once more, through her bedroom window, she watched as the perimeter rainbow danced and the brilliant bulk of the alien vessel hovered white and unmoving. As if waiting for her, again, to come outside and pray to it.

But she did not know if she trusted the saucer's commander any more than she trusted her own suicidal tendencies.

Why had it transported her back to Jerry's grave?

Was hell on Mars, and heaven on Venus?

Did the space commander know Jerry?

"Do you know where Jerry is?"

Yes. The Ouija board had said yes.

Yet she hadn't enjoyed the seance.

She didn't trust Pamela's motives for holding it.

She hadn't killed Jerry. God had killed him.

"Go to hell," she whispered to the flying saucer.

Perhaps to God as well.

Mary returned to bed and fell asleep.

13

The next day Mary went to work at Seedmont's only theater, where she was an usher as well as a popcorn popper. She'd had the job for over a year. Savey had got it for her. His uncle owned the place, which was ironic because the uncle was blind. But no one loved movies more than old Mr. Barker. He could listen to them for hours. He especially liked the sound of special effects and could tell the good ones from the cheap ones.

When everyone was seated for the matinee, Mary tried to talk with Mr. Barker about the previous night. He was busy counting the money, as he always did during previews. He was a lousy businessman. If a kid showed up without money to get into the theater, Mr. Barker always extended him credit. He estimated that since he'd opened the theater forty years ago he had lent out a quarter of a million dollars in tickets. That was why his coat was old and shabby and he lived in an apartment where his toaster oven doubled as a stove. He was ancient and close to death but he was a content old fart. Mary didn't understand him at all, but she liked him a great deal.

No one had mentioned a flying saucer visiting Seedmont the previous night. Yet both of Mary's robes were dirty in the morning. The filthiest dream could not have left actual dirt. That was a physical fact—even if she was losing her mind.

"Mr. Barker," Mary said. "Do you believe there's life on other planets?"

He looked up at her with his blind eyes. They were both glass, actually, unnerving, and when he stared at her she always felt she had to pee. But he seemed to know that, so he didn't look at her too long. He returned to counting the change, and then the dollars. He could tell a one from a five, don't ask how.

"Are you talking about life on other planets in this solar system?" he asked.

"I suppose."

"Then my answer would be no. Mars had the best shot at having life, besides Earth, but it's beginning to look like it can't even support microbes. None of the other planets or moons comes close to having enough oxygen or water to keep anything alive."

"What about planets in other solar systems?"

"You mean around other stars?"

"Yes."

He whistled. "I would say yes, definitely. There are four hundred billion stars in our galaxy alone. And there are billions of galaxies that we have seen with our telescopes. To believe we're the only planet in the entire universe to have developed life would be rather arrogant of us, don't you think?"

"Yes." She paused. "Do you think any of these aliens have visited us?"

"What aliens?"

"The ones, you know, out there."

He looked at her once more. "What put these questions in your mind, Mary? Have you seen a flying saucer?"

"Yes."

Since he couldn't see, and was open-minded, he was all ears. Tell me about it, he said. So she told him as many details as she could without revealing that it had become her habit to go the cemetery at night and lie on top of her dead boyfriend's grave. She feared it might offend his sensibilities. When she was finished Mr. Barker was quiet and very thoughtful.

"I won't ask you if you were dreaming," he said. "I know you're too bright not to be able to tell the difference. But let me ask you something, and please don't get offended."

"I won't get offended as long as you don't bring up Jerry."

Mr. Barker blinked, which he did only when he was uncomfortable. "That could be part of it, I'm sorry to have to say. When you've gone through what you've had to cope with, it's hard not to start seeing things."

She spoke bluntly without a trace of meanness.

"You don't think I was dreaming, but you do think I might have been hallucinating?"

He held up a hand. "You say no one else appears to have seen this saucer."

"It was late. I don't know how long it was there."

"Are there any physical signs that it was here? Burned bushes or trees—that sort of thing."

"I didn't say it landed." She hesitated. "I told you about my robes."

Mr. Barker was shrewd. "You were vague on that point. Where did this saucer teleport you?"

She didn't know what to say, except the truth.

"To the cemetery. But it doesn't mean Jerry's involved."

"If it doesn't then it's a hell of a coincidence," Mr. Barker said.

She started to argue with him. But then realized he was right.

14

That night she had a dream. She was in a desert with a friend. She couldn't see his face and didn't know what her own looked like. The sun was incredibly bright. It felt as if it were twice as close to the Earth as normal. She knew that was the name of the planet they were on, the third one from the star—from the sun.

They spotted several people in the distance, a caravan of sorts, being transported on domesticated beasts. The beasts were camels. They could see these people but the people couldn't see them. Not unless she wished it. She wanted to communicate with them; they seemed interesting to her, more beautiful than she or her companion. But her friend was against the idea. Yet she reigned supreme. She was the commander.

Mysteriously she made herself visible.

Seeing them, the humans cried in terror.

But as she walked toward them, she became them. Even more so. More beautiful and more charming.

They calmed down and worshipped her.

She liked that. Very much.

She loved the way she looked now.

Her companion was concerned.

She didn't want to return home now.

And she didn't. Ever.

15

Mary woke up in the dark and listened to her heart. It beat steadily, and her lungs moved in and out. She was human. She was not the creature in the dream.

You thought you were a god.

The Ouija board had put some weird ideas in her brain.

Of course, they had not talked about flying saucers at the seance.

Mary sat up and dialed Savey. Glancing at her clock, she saw it was one in the morning. He answered after eight rings.

"Hello?"

"Savey, it's me. I need you to come over."

"OK." He paused. "Are your parents still away?"

"Yeah. Pick up Ken on the way. Have him bring his Ouija board."

A longer pause. "I don't get it."

"I want to have another seance."

He sounded annoyed. "You can wake me up in the middle of the night to have sex. Not to have a seance."

"Please, it's important. Strange things have been going on."

"What kind of strange things?"

"I'll tell you. Just come."

16

Savey looked as if he had been awakened from death when he got to her house. But Ken appeared fresh. She doubted that he had even been to bed. He came through her door with the Ouija board in his hands. Her late night request had not caught him off guard.

"Has something been trying to contact you?" he asked.

"Yes," she said.

Once again, she explained about the flying saucer, once again leaving out the part about lying on top of Jerry's grave. She worried that her nasty habit would distract from the credibility of her tale. She didn't mention her dream either. Ken listened closely. Savey kept yawning. When she was done, she didn't wait for either of their comments.

"Now tell me what you and Pamela were up to before the party," she said to Ken.

"The week before we had been fooling around with the Ouija board and talked with that same being who spoke the night of the party. We asked about Jerry and it brought up your name a couple of times." Ken shrugged. "That's all there is to it."

"Why were you using a Ouija board in the first place?" Mary said. "And why did Pamela get it in her head that I was responsible for Jerry's death?"

Ken thought before answering. "I felt something near."

"What do you mean?" Savey asked, finally waking up.

"Ever since we buried Jerry, I've felt something near me," Ken said. "I know it sounds weird but I often feel it."

"Is it Jerry's soul, do you think?" Mary asked.

Ken shook his head. "I don't know. It feels familiar. But it doesn't seem exactly like my brother."

"Why was Pamela on my case?" Mary repeated.

Ken caught her eye. "It wasn't just the things spelled out on the Ouija board that made us wonder about that night."

Mary met his gaze. "What do you wonder, Ken? You know I didn't kill Jerry."

"Were you there?" he asked seriously.

She paused. "Maybe."

Savey was astounded. "Mary! You lied to the police?"

" 'You lie. She lies. All lie,' " she quoted.

Ken leaned forward and spoke with feeling. "I just want to know why my brother died. That's all I want. I won't tell anyone. Not even my parents. Please, Mary."

She hesitated. "The guard shot him."

Savey was impatient. "We know the guard shot him. Who shot the guard?"

"He shot himself," Mary said.

"Why would he shoot himself?" Savey asked.

"You mean, he shot himself accidentally?" Ken said. "Is that what you're saying?"

"Yes."

"Was there a struggle?" Ken asked.

"Yes."

"And the gun went off?" Ken asked.

"Yes."

"Did the guard intend to shoot my brother?" Ken asked.

Mary lowered her head. "He shot him in the arm. But I don't think he would have intentionally shot him in the head."

"Was Jerry involved in this struggle?" Ken asked.

"Not directly," Mary said.

"Why were you both there?" Ken asked.

Mary raised her head. "I didn't say I was there. I said maybe I was there."

"All right," Savey interrupted. "We understand. Hypothetically, why were you maybe there?"

"To count the homecoming queen ballots." Mary looked at both of them. "I know, Jerry was a great guy, and there should have been a better reason for him to die. It just happened so fast." She swallowed thickly. "It won't do any good for me to say I'm sorry."

Ken sat back in his chair and drew in a deep breath. Savey stared at her and shook his head. There were tears in both the guys' eyes. But there were none in hers.

When Ken finally spoke it was with difficulty. "Why do you want to use the Ouija board now?"

"I want to talk to the guy on the spaceship," Mary said.

"It might be better to contact NASA," Savey suggested sarcastically, still reeling from Mary's revelations.

"The saucer showed up after the seance," Ken said. "Is that what you mean?"

She nodded. "Yes. We assumed we were talking to a spirit. But maybe we were talking to an alien."

"We were delving into our collective subconscious," Savey said. "Nothing more."

"Which is the same as saying nothing," Ken said. He gestured to his board. "Let's try it again. I'm game."

Savey shook his head and sighed. "I can't believe I'm here for this reason." But then he looked at her and his face softened. Perhaps he realized how hard it had been for her to keep the truth bottled up inside. How much she must trust both of them to blurt it out now. He added, "I'll write down what comes through, but I'm not joining in. It won't bring Jerry back."

Mary went for candles and Ken cleared off the dining room table. Savey found a note pad in the kitchen. Ten minutes later they were ready to speak to the friendly spirits.

As before, the planchette started by describing tiny circles that steadily grew in size. Soon the indicator was all over the board. Tonight the energy was more concentrated, more focused. Already, even before it began to speak, Mary felt that same peculiar charge at the base of her spine. Slowly, it moved upward toward her head. They weren't even given a chance to inquire before the planchette began to spell out a message.

> *All are doomed to burn.*
> *Love feeds the flames.*
> *Days of endless pains.*
> *And the smoke takes each in turn.*
>
> *All are doomed to rust.*
> *Time destroys our lives.*
> *Nights cut like knives.*
> *And the wind carries away the dust.*
>
> *All are doomed to love.*
> *All are doomed to die.*
> *Tonight bring the black tomb.*
> *For even the most high.*
> *Even those in this room.*
> *Cannot pretend to fly*
> *And I know.*
> *Even you.*
> *Even I.*
> *Must die.*

They sat in silence for a minute after Savey read the entire message.

"What the hell is that?" Ken finally whispered.

The Ouija board told them.

Prayer of the false God.

"Is it from ancient Egypt?" Ken asked.

Yes.

"Was it known in that time?" Ken asked.

During a certain period.

"Why do you tell it to us?"

A warning.

"Are we really in danger?" Ken asked.

Yes.

"Why?"

Mystery.

"Is it because of me?" Mary asked, her spine arching slightly, like that of a cat.

Yes.

"Why?" Mary asked. "What will I do?"

Mystery.

"Will she do what she did before?" Ken asked. "In ancient Egypt?"

It hesitated.

Close.

"Can this danger happen without you?" Ken asked.

No.

"Then why don't you go away?" Ken asked.

I am drawn.

"To me?" Mary whispered.

Something was vibrating inside her. Something unnatural.

It hesitated.

Yes.

"But why?" Mary demanded.

It hesitated.

Mystery.

"What is the black tomb?" Ken asked.

The life seemed to go out of the room.

A nightmare.

Mary felt a painful pop in her spine. The energy stopped.

Then the being was gone, and they couldn't get it back. No matter how much they pleaded. "Too bad," Ken said. "I was just going to ask it about the flying saucer."

Mary shifted uneasily. Her spine was cold now, sore. It felt as if she had been given an electroshock treatment. "I don't like this prayer."

"It's more of a poem," Savey said, studying it. "But I don't see how it warns us of anything."

Ken spoke to her. "Mary, I appreciate your coming straight with us. Now I'm going to ask you to do it again." He paused. "Have you been up to anything unusual lately?"

"I haven't slept with Savey, if that's what you're asking."

"I don't think I was included in the question," Savey said, annoyed.

Ken was serious. "We have to let Jerry go," he said to her.

"You're the one who went to the toy store and bought the Ouija board," Mary said.

"I know," Ken said. "That was probably a mistake. But what I mean is, whatever this danger is supposed to be, it's connected to *your* connection to Jerry."

"Who just happens to be dead and completely out of the way," Savey said.

"You're always so sarcastic," Ken told him.

"I am always reasonable," Savey said. "Which is more than I can say for you guys. There is no danger. There are no aliens. We're all just screwed up because

Jerry is no longer here. It's as simple and painful as that." He stood. "Now I'm going home and going to bed."

"I dreamed about Egypt tonight," Mary said, staring down at the Ouija board.

"What did you dream?" Ken asked.

"That I was special." Mary paused. "What does the word *akasha* mean?"

"Never heard of it," Savey snapped. "Let's go, Ken."

"It means space or ether," Ken said. "It's often used when referring to the akashic records."

"What are those?" Mary asked.

"The supposedly imperishable records of everything that's ever happened in the universe. Our every word and deed—from thousands of incarnations on this planet—is recorded in the akashic records." Ken paused. "Why do you ask about the word?"

"It was one of the last things Jerry said to me before he died," Mary said.

"What did he say?" Ken asked. "Specifically?"

Mary stared at the Ouija board. "He said the akasha burns."

Ken was intrigued, confused. "Anything else?"

"No," she lied. They all lied, sometime.

17

The guys left and Mary returned to bed. Soon she was asleep, but rest was not synonymous with her unconscious state. She felt as if she were working even in sleep. Something hard and heavy lay on top of her, a thick marble covering, and she seemed to struggle forever to get it off. But it never went away. It just wore down, as the flesh on her fingers wore down. She was bleeding, and in constant pain.

No one could hear her screams.

Or if they could, they didn't care.

18

Mary sat up in bed, awake. The white light was back. It flooded her bedroom like a million-watt torch wired to the Las Vegas Strip. In the stark rays that pierced through her curtains, she saw fresh bloodstains on her sheets. Yet her fingers were undamaged. They just ached a little.

Mary stood and walked to the window.

The spaceship floated directly above her house.

"I am not dreaming this," she whispered.

Mary grabbed her phone and dialed Savey's number.

The person who answered was not Savey, however.

"Yes, Clareesh?" the voice said. She wasn't even sure of the sex of the voice. The tone was extraordinarily soft, powerful as well, but not necessarily with human strengths. The voice could have been artificial in origin, the smoothly recited syllables of a computer so highly developed it was almost a blasphemy to the idea that God had created man in His own image.

She froze. "Who is this?"

"It is all the same person, Clareesh."

This is my phone! It isn't a goddamn Ouija board.

But she couldn't hang up. Not without an answer.

"Who is Clareesh?" she whispered.

"The sacrifice. The sacrificer. It is all the same person, Clareesh."

She trembled. "It's all me?"

"You are what you are," it agreed.

"What do you want with me?"

Was it an echo? "What do you want with me?"

"Nothing! I just want Jerry back!"

The voice hesitated, which was strange for something so alien to do. It was not so sure of itself, after all. "Then you want what you want, Clareesh." It added faintly, almost too faint to hear, "The nightmare goes on and on."

"Wait!" Mary screamed into the phone. "Don't leave!"

"Hello?"

Again, Mary froze. "Who is this?"

The voice was sleepy. "Savey. What do you want, Mary?"

"Did you just pick up the phone? This second?"

"Yes."

"How many times did it ring before you picked it up?"

"I don't know. I was asleep. What is it with you tonight?"

Mary spoke quietly. "It's here."

"What's here?"

Mary realized it was dark in her bedroom. She hurried to the window, still clutching the phone. "It's gone," she gasped.

Savey was sarcastic. "It's here. It's gone. Anything else?"

She spoke like a machine. "No. Go back to sleep, Savey."

"Thank you." He hung up.

Mary changed her sheets and went back to bed.

If she dreamed, her conscious mind found it too horrible to recall.

19

The next night, Sunday, Mary went for a long walk in the woods behind her house. She brought a flashlight, a thermos of coffee. It was very cold and dark; she meant only to go out for an hour or two but she ended up walking so far she came to the spot where she had first fallen in love with Jerry.

There, crouched at the side of the clearing, was an alien.

It looked like one of the creatures from the supermarket tabloids. The kind with the tiny gray bodies, the large heads, the huge black emotionless eyes. The kind of creature that was supposed to abduct people in the middle of the night and perform medical experiments on them. The kind that always showed up in hypnotherapy regression sessions. The cause of half the childhood abuse problems in the nation, according to some experts. Nasty buggers, with their anal probes and lousy bedside manners.

Mary stared at the creature for an eternity.

It watched her. The little guy.

E.T. never had eyes like this thing. Besides being large, almond shaped, and black as coal, they were bottomless. As she stared into them, Mary felt as if she fell through space and time to a place where the wisdom of the ages was stored. A place without boundaries or definition, that knew the meaning of violent cruelty as well as unconditional love, and saw no conflict in these two extremes. The creature's eyes were truly windows into another dimension. Just to stand near them, to it, was to feel enveloped in mystery.

Mystery.

Mary finally managed a smile, a single word. "Hello."

It opened its mouth to respond. Then hissed.

Something large and hungry snarled at her back.

Mary spun around and caught a black bear in the beam of her flashlight.

A mother bear with cubs. The kind that killed.

Mary screamed and dropped her light and ran.

The bear chased her, she could hear it. But its snarls changed to those of a pack of wolves as it closed. Then there was the flapping of bats wings over her head. The swarm of vampiric birds smelled her blood. They were thirsty; she could tell by the dryness of their acidic saliva as it dripped onto her hair. She couldn't stop screaming. Yet as she finally burst from the woods, onto a man-made road, she realized there was nothing behind her or above her. Just her past, still in front of her.

She never did find her flashlight, or her thermos.

20

School the next morning was boring. Until Mary heard word of a new kid on campus. His name was Tom, and the contagious rumors were that he was way cool. Mary had yet to meet him when she bumped into Pamela at lunch. But Pamela took time and care to describe him in detail. It seemed that Pamela had magically forgotten that the previous Friday she had accused Mary of murder. Mary didn't hold it against her, for the moment. She was curious about the guy.

"Does he have a cute butt?" Mary asked.

"He looks like sex with all the trimmings! His hair is so blond, his eyes so blue—you just want to take him home and stuff him! And he has the most darling smile! I think I'm in love!"

"Well, if he's that great I'll probably keep him for myself."

Pamela's face darkened. "I saw him first."

"It's who sees him last that counts."

Pamela was angry. "You already stole one boyfriend from me. And look what happened."

Mary put a finger in Pamela's face. "You watch your mouth you also-ran princess. I didn't appreciate that little stunt you pulled at your party."

Pamela was not apologetic, to say the least. "I know you shot one of them. I don't know why you just don't admit it."

Mary slapped her in the face. "I shot both of them. Then I licked up the blood. Are you happy?"

Pamela didn't strike back. She had blood on her lip, but grinned wickedly. "I think Tom's already mine. He doesn't look like the type who goes in for psychopaths."

Mary glanced around. "Where is he?"

Pamela sneered. "Like I'm going to tell you?"

"Like you know." Mary patted Pamela on the back. "Later, bitch."

21

Mary didn't meet Tom that day but the next. She saw him after school in the parking lot as she walked toward her car. He didn't seem to be going to a car. He was strolling as if he had a hundred years to reach home. That was the first thing she liked about Tom, the way he moved. He just seemed to float along. She hurried toward him.

He was dressed simply in blue jeans, a long-sleeved white shirt, and jacket. As Pamela had observed, he had gorgeous white-blond hair. The day was overcast but the sun still granted him a special spotlight. He was deeply tanned, so tan that the color appeared genetic. Although on the thin side, he appeared to be strong. Graceful, either in complete control of his surroundings or absolutely oblivious to them.

"Hello," she called.

He paused and turned. The gaze from his blue eyes seemed to *pass through her* before focusing on her. It was an odd sensation but Mary liked it. He smiled; he had nice teeth.

"Hello," he said.

She moved closer, offered her hand. "My name's Mary Weist. You must be Tom."

He shook her hand smoothly. Although his skin tones and build were quite different, he reminded her of Jerry. He was wearing sandals, she realized. Plain leather sandals on a frigid November day. He didn't look cold, though.

"I'm Tom," he said.

She smiled. "So you're the new kid in school. I've heard a lot about you."

"What have you heard?"

She blushed. "Well, Pamela Poole said you had a nice butt." She added, "Do you know her?"

He nodded. "We've met. She's a cheerleader."

"Yeah. I'm not one of those." She brightened. "But I am homecoming queen. That's pretty impressive, don't you think?"

He laughed, and it seemed as if he did so despite himself. There was something serious about new boy Tom. He didn't look like a flake.

"Are you trying to impress me, Mary?" he asked.

Again she felt blood in her cheeks. "No, I just wanted to meet you." She gestured in the direction he was heading. "Can I give you a ride home?"

He considered. "You don't have to."

She shrugged. "It's no problem. I'm going that way anyway."

He appeared puzzled. "Which way is that?"

She turned toward her car. "Anywhere away from here."

22

They ended up stopping at the local Denny's. Mary hadn't eaten all day and Tom was agreeable to having something. But after studying the menu, all he ordered was a glass of milk.

"Is that all you're having?" she asked. She was going to have a burger and fries, which was going to be hard to stuff in her mouth when the guy sitting across from her was on a diet. But Tom's decision was not set in stone.

"What are you going to have?" he asked.

She told him.

"I'll have that, too," he told the waitress.

The waitress took their menus and left to put their order in. Mary had to laugh.

"If I jump off a cliff, are you going to follow me?" she asked.

Concern touched his face. "Are you going to jump, Mary?"

She lost her smile. "I suppose you've heard about me as well?"

He nodded. "Pamela told me that your boyfriend died last month."

"Did she tell you that I killed him?"

"No."

"That's good. It's not true. He was shot in the head by a security guard at school. What's ironic is that the guard committed suicide immediately afterward. Don't you think that's strange?"

"You must miss him very much."

Mary shrugged. "Shit happens. Jerry knew what he was doing when he broke into the office and tried to alter the ballots voting me homecoming queen." She stopped and laughed. "That's a sick joke. You see, Tom, half the school believes I forced Jerry to go to the school that night. Don't you think that's strange?"

"Yes."

"This is a strange town. You live here a while you'll see all kinds of interesting things. Believe me, I know. Hey, do you like movies?"

"Yes."

"I work at the movie theater. I can get you in free, anytime. Just ask for me. The theater owner is blind, but he's a great guy. He acts like I'm his favorite daughter." She paused. "Am I rambling?"

Tom shook his head. "You're just being you."

23

Mary never did take Tom home. Later, much later, after a long walk in the woods, they ended up back at her place. By then it was dark and freezing. Mary suggested they build a fire, and Tom, as always, was amenable. Soon they had such a huge blaze going it could have competed with the meltdown Savey had spawned the night of the party. Just the thought of that evening made Mary want to take off her clothes. She had just met Tom, though, and didn't want him to get the wrong idea about her. It was just that she felt so comfortable around him, and he hardly said a word. Really, when she talked to him, she felt as if she were yacking to a mirror. And you couldn't be too shy in front of a mirror.

She didn't know for sure who kissed who first, but she was ninety percent sure it was she who was the initiator. Not that Tom held back once he had her in his arms. Ten minutes at the outside and they were both naked and rolling on the carpet on the floor in front of the fire. He had an awesome body, better than Jerry's, twice as good as Savey's, what she had seen of it. Even better than her own. Yet, when it was time to have intercourse, he stopped and sat up and stared at the fire. She had never had a boy do that before. She touched his shoulder.

"What's the matter?" she asked.

"I can't," he said.

She looked him over. "I think you can." She paused. "I have a condom. I was just going to get it."

He smiled slightly, the orange light caressing his perfect profile. "That isn't a problem. I just don't think we should make love tonight. You are still too upset about Jerry. You have no love and we'll end up making nothing."

"And we'll end up feeling worse than before," she whispered, echoing her line to Savey from the other night. "How did you know I felt that way?"

He looked through her then as he did when they first met.

"Because I know you—Mary," he said.

She froze. "You were going to call me something else. What were you going to call me?"

Tom turned back to the fire. He didn't answer.

24

The next day at school they had lunch together in the central courtyard. Half the student body watched, from a discreet distance. Mary didn't mind the attention. Tom had what she had, a turkey sandwich and potato chips. She had packed it for him that morning.

They didn't talk much.

25

That night Mary was sleeping alone when the flying saucer returned. Opening her eyes and seeing the bright light flooding her room, she wondered if she should bother getting out of bed. She knew she would just have another transcendental experience and feel lousy about it in the morning. Yet, curiousity killed the cat and the love of her life, and so in the end she rose and padded over to the window. The moment she did, the light and ship vanished.

Yet it had left something behind.

The little alien stood in the center of her backyard.

Mary put on her clean woolen robe and went outside.

It looked over at her with those big black eyes.

"Hello." She waved briefly. "Nice to see you again."

The alien seemed to smile, although its tiny mouth hardly moved. It had no lips. It held out one of its large gray hands. Four fingers, no thumb. It wanted to touch her.

"All right," she said softly.

Mary took a step forward, held out her own hand. It felt as if the ship returned right then, above her head, but she didn't bother to check. The eyes of the alien were all she saw. Those black pools of wonder. It was strange how something so black could shine with such luster.

Their hands touched.
The light escalated, obliterating everything else.
The akasha burned.
Everything changed for her.

26

"Don't go, Clareesh," Klaxtor said, holding on to her hand.

Clareesh stood enthralled by the line of advancing humans, hardly aware of her partner. "They are so primitive," she said. "Who would have thought they could be so attractive."

"We are here to observe, nothing more."

Clareesh glanced at Klaxtor. "I say what we are here to do."

Klaxtor nodded out of respect. "That is your right. But you have only earned that right through repeated demonstrations of wisdom. If you make contact with the humans, you will lose your rank and your vessel."

Clareesh chuckled as she turned back to observe the caravan. There were ten camels and twenty of the humans—fifteen men and five females. She thought it amusing that the females were forced to walk, when they were obviously the weaker sex. So primitive indeed, these humans. The females also carried the heavier baggage. Beneath the burning sun, laboring over the windswept sand dunes, they had no easy chore. The inequity was one thing she would like to correct, before they departed. She shook off Klaxtor's hand.

"No one will talk about what I do this day," she warned him.

Klaxtor was concerned. "What are you going to do?"

"Make friends."

"It is well known in this sector that human friendships do not endure."

She stepped toward the humans. "We will see, Klaxtor. Remain here until I return."

Here was in the vicinity of their spaceship. But that also was not visible to the human beings. Because people on Earth were only evolved to third density. The animals and plants of Earth were second density. The rocks and other minerals were first density. Clareesh and her partner were fourth density. If they wished, they could vibrate both their ship and their bodies down to a lower plane, if a situation warranted it. But they were only to do so under the most pressing circumstances, when the Law of Life was threatened. Of course, they could vibrate no higher than fourth density, no matter what the situation.

"I will wait for you," Klaxtor promised.

Clareesh walked in the direction of the human caravan. As she did so, she drew in deep breaths of the Earth's atmosphere. It was the subtle life force in the breath, the *prana,* that allowed her to become part of the planet's normal vibratory rate. She merely needed to direct the air and energy, and she would become visible to them.

This seemed to happen all at once for the humans.

When they saw her, saw what she looked like, they screamed.

Their reaction troubled Clareesh. To her, form was

not so important as it was to these creatures enmeshed in third degree matter. She could change her appearance at will. Yet their shape intrigued her, it was the primary reason she wished to make contact. She wanted to find out more about their bodies, what they could do, how they reacted to the environment, to one another. For a little while, she wanted to be human.

Focusing on one of the terrified females, Clareesh froze the woman in place. Then Clareesh began to shape shift. Soon she looked identical to the young woman.

The scattering group froze. A hush went through them.

Clareesh had their attention, and now it was not all bad. Slowly, she began to scan each of their minds, searching for what was their ideal of female beauty. When she had a reasonable composite, she shape shifted once again.

This time they fell to their knees. All except one.

The female whose form she had originally copied refused to bow.

Clareesh reached out and studied her mind. Her name was Phairee; she was a servant in a high priest's house. This priest was one of the most powerful men in the nearby civilization that flourished by the river known as the Nile. The priest was abusive; he both beat and sexually violated Phairee. She often thought of killing him. Phairee was intelligent and proud. She did not trust this new god who had just appeared. She thought Clareesh might be worse than the last one. Clareesh stepped toward her and spoke telepathically to the young woman.

"Who was the last one?" she asked.

Phairee took a step back, but never flinched.

"It was long ago," she said quietly. "I never met him, but he caused many people to be sacrificed to the sun. These sacrifices continue to this day."

Clareesh smiled. *"Believe me Phairee, today they end."*

Clareesh glanced back in the direction of Klaxtor. Having lowered herself to a third density body, she could not see him now. Not with her limited human eyes. But she could sense his presence—and his disapproval. And she had, in fact, not lost all remembrance of her race's rules about contacting primitive species. She had no intention of greatly modifying the existing culture—she just wanted to play with it for a brief time, bring a ray of enlightenment to it. How could her superiors condemn her for stopping human sacrifice? The Law of Life was higher than their manufactured laws.

Phairee had reached out to touch her hand.

"Are you really a god?" she asked.

Clareesh took a deep breath, enjoying her new body, the many delicious sensations it gave her. Even the touch of Phairee's hand on her own was wonderful. She patted the young woman on the head.

"I am your goddess," she said in the woman's mind.

They took her back to their city, to the huge pyramids by the Nile, the crowning achievement of human civilization. Clareesh could see the influence of a higher race in the structure of the stone buildings, yet she did not believe it was connected to her own people. It was a mystery; perhaps the earlier evil god had commanded them to be built.

Phairee presented Clareesh to the high priest as a goddess sent to their world to teach them love and kindness. Clareesh enjoyed the introduction, and clearly the high priest relished the sight of her, although his mind was already working out how he would control and use her beauty to solidify his position. Clareesh wasted no time in destroying his illusions. As he stepped down from his magnificent golden chair to greet her, Clareesh raised her hand and surrounded him in a circle of towering fire.

That was her first miracle in ancient Egypt.

It caused a sensation.

Overnight Clareesh became the people's reigning deity.

Many years passed, but they didn't seem many to her because to all intents and purposes, she was immortal. But each new year she thought of returning to her home in the sky. The longing was there; it would come upon her when the stars were especially bright. And for the people of Egypt, she had already done much good, much that she could be proud of. No longer did they need to fear being killed for the sake of invisible gods. There was justice now that she was the only judge. Their systems of agriculture and writing and medicine she advanced many centuries. Yes, she knew it was close to the time to return home.

Yet every year she had a new excuse for not leaving. There were many things about being human that she enjoyed: the taste of food and wine; the feel of fine silk on her skin; the beauty of the sun when it first rose. At dawn she would walk along the river and try to remember what it had been like to be locked inside a spaceship, traveling from world to empty world.

Sometimes she had trouble remembering, because the longer she stayed third density, the more she lost her fourth density abilities. For example, after thirty years of being in the pyramid city, she could no longer read human minds. The loss of control disturbed her, but there were many compensations.

Always, she thought, she would leave the following year.

She knew Klaxtor waited for her signal.

Phairee had become her personal assistant. Phairee had been lucky to get the position. Only three days after Clareesh first entered the city, Phairee slit the high priest's throat while he slept. Clareesh had almost banished Phairee to the desert that same day, but the young woman wept and pleaded for mercy. And Clareesh understood the torment Phairee had suffered at the priest's hands. She had granted her a pardon, and steadily Phairee had earned her confidence. Phairee was a tireless worker. She loved to take charge of a project, and see it through to the end. At present she was one of the most powerful people in the kingdom.

Yet Phairee was not totally satisfied with her lot in life.

Thirty years had passed since Clareesh had come.

Clareesh had not aged, but Phairee was now a middle-aged woman.

"Is there not some way," Phairee occasionally said to her, "that you could reveal to me your secret of immortality?"

"I have told you," Clareesh said. "Your nature and mine are not the same. You evolve through many lives. That is proper for you. It is what you really want, deep down. For example, if you wore the same garment every day, you would soon tire of it. In the same way, you cast off this body when you are finished with it and you are given another. There is no difference."

Phairee gestured to her body. "But I like this garment. I don't want it to die."

"There is no death. You will see. On the other side you will be met with a bright light and you will be glad."

Phairee acted puzzled. "Will I meet you there?"

"No. Our paths are different. That is one aspect of the Law of Life. We must have respect for each other's differences."

Phairee would nod in understanding and go away, apparently satisfied. But some months later she would ask the same questions, and each time Clareesh found it harder to satisfy her concern about her aging body. Phairee was rather vain; she could not bear to see wrinkles in the mirror. To that Clareesh was sympathetic. She still loved the form she had adopted that day she bid Klaxtor goodbye. It had grown on her. She coveted it more than the powers she had forfeited.

After thirty-five years of living as a human, Clareesh one morning came upon a young man sculpting an image of her. She had never seen this man before. He was not a member of the prized guild that she had founded to encourage the arts. Yet his sculpture was extraordinary. Staring at it, Clareesh saw a mirror in stone that captured her depth. Studying the young man, she felt a wonder she had never known before. She invited him to walk with her along the Nile and he humbly accepted.

His name was Jarteen, and he cared for sheep and goats with his aged father in the hills around the city. His sculpting was self taught; he had no teacher. In Clareesh's mind, that made his statue of her all the more remarkable. Not all her powers were lost. She saw in his eyes a light she had only seen in the center of the galaxy, where the many colored stars crowded so close together that the entire sky shone like a living jewel. That morning she invited both him and his father to stay with her.

"You will develop your talent to its fullest," she said. "And perhaps we can meet and talk on occasion."

They ended up talking every day, and night. Besides being unable to read minds, Clareesh could no longer telepathically impress thoughts on humans. But it seemed with Jarteen that she had met a third density soul that vibrated far beyond what the Law of Life would normally dictate. They communicated as if through osmosis. She just needed to be near him.

The need grew quickly. His physical beauty and talent astounded her. But it was his gentle heart that broke her heart. He worshipped her unconditionally. He asked for nothing in return. Such a love, in her mind, could not go unacknowledged. But she accepted it in a manner she had sworn at the beginning of her entry into the city that she never would do. She fell in love with Jarteen.

He became her lover.

Her superiors would never forgive the transgression, she knew. She, a fourth density being, having sex with a third density creature. It violated the very core of the Law of Life. Oh, but she could not help herself. For too long she had been without intimate contact. When Jarteen caressed her, she felt as if she floated in the vast void of intergalactic space. She believed Jarteen gave her back what she had surrendered to be human. Yet, ironically, he bound her more firmly to the world that she was supposed to leave soon.

They were lovers six months when they were found out.

Phairee, with a squad of heavily armed attendants, came upon them naked in bed together in Clareesh's bed chamber. Clareesh had assumed Phairee's guards were as loyal to her as her own, but looking into their twisted dull faces, she realized Phairee had used evil medicinal arts to pervert their minds and dominate their wills. Each carried a torch and a sword. Phairee carried a sharp knife and knelt on the edge of the bed to hold the blade against Clareesh's throat.

"Tell me about the Law of Life," Phairee said in a deadly tone. "Tell me, my goddess, what is allowed and what is forbidden?"

Clareesh had long ago surrendered the special abilities that could repel any human attack. Sitting naked beside Jarteen, she was quite helpless. Phairee seemed to know that; she was always shrewd.

"All you have, I gave to you," Clareesh told her. "Is this how you repay me?"

Phairee sneered. "But you do not give me all you have! Again and again you have said you and humans could never mingle. And now we find you have broken your most sacred commandment." She gestured to her dull-faced guards. "What are we to think?"

Clareesh caught her eye. "You dare to judge me? How many lovers did you have last month? How many will you have in the coming month?"

Phairee raged. "But I don't call myself a goddess! I don't pretend to be worshipped! Not like you, Clareesh, you hypocrite!"

Clareesh spoke calmly. "What are you setting yourself up for? To take my place as ruler of this land?"

Phairee smiled then, and withdrew her blade an inch. "If I was the ruler, I could allow this transgression to pass unpunished." She leaned close and added, "If you give me the secret, I will do this for you. Jarteen may go with you, wherever you choose to go."

Clareesh snorted softly. "You can offer nothing. I am the ruler here, not you."

Phairee's smile widened. She gestured to her guards. "Who rules this bedroom, Clareesh? I think it must be clear that it is me. And since all you have and all you love is in this room, then you must accept my offer. Make me immortal, and then leave the city quietly."

Clareesh sighed. "I have told you many times, I cannot alter your basic nature."

Phairee lost her smile. "You have also lied to me many times! I think this is just another of those times." She nodded to Jarteen. "Why, I suspect you have already granted your handsome lover the secret of everlasting life. Yes, I think I will put my theory to the test." She gestured to the guards. "Spread him on his back on the floor."

"No!" Clareesh cried. "He is no more immortal than you are! If you cut him he will bleed!"

Phairee gestured bitterly with her blade. "If he bleeds it is your fault! You can save him and yourself. You can save me. I have served you for many years. Yet you let me grow old and ugly while you continue to parade your beauty in front of the masses. I tell you, I will not stand for it. If I am to die, all will die." She paused to catch her breath. Once more she pressed the blade to Clareesh's throat. "Give me the secret, goddess. This is your last chance."

Clareesh spoke with sorrow. "All right, I will tell you my race's great secret. The one parcel of knowledge that leads to eternity for all creatures, no matter what their level of development. But I have told it to you before. It is nothing new. There is nothing new under the sun."

"Damnit!" Phairee swore. "What is it?"

"You must have love. For all creatures high and low. You must find this love in your own heart, and then see that love everywhere." Clareesh paused and felt a tear run over her cheek. She had never wept before. The knife felt cold against her flesh. This is what she should have taught humanity from the beginning, nothing else. "You must be kind, merciful, and above all else, accepting of what you are. Because you are as you were created, and in the beginning of all things the creator made you perfect in his eyes." She wiped away the tear. "That is the greatest secret I can tell you, Phairee. You know in your heart, that all these years, I have loved you. Do what you want to me, but please let Jarteen go. He has done you no harm."

Phairee drew back. Her expression was difficult to read. For a moment it was as if she was filled with a mad joy. Her wrinkled lips fastened in a bizarre smile.

But then the remnant of joy vanished and there was just madness. She screamed to her guards.

"Spread him on the floor! We will open him up and see what she has put inside!"

Clareesh could not bear to watch, but she did. She was a goddess, after all, a supposed protector of those in dire need. Jarteen looked to her as Phairee knelt by his side with her blade poised. His throat was too choked with fear for him to speak, but his eyes told her that he forgave her. That loving her, even for a few months, had been worth the loss of his life. All these things, this unconditional love, she clearly saw.

"I feel the same way," she said aloud.

Phairee went to work with her knife.

Jarteen screamed. And Phairee laughed.

There was so much blood, for so long.

Jarteen died slowly and in great pain.

Then Phairee commanded her guards to take Jarteen's lifeless body and Clareesh, and bury them together in a tomb far beneath a pyramid. In a black tomb that only she had the key to. Down they carried Clareesh, through tunnels in the great pyramid that even she did not know, their torches burning, their cries delirious.

Clareesh was dumped in a thick stone box with only the blood soaked body of her lover for company. Although she fought with every last bit of her strength in her arms and legs, she was unable to stop them from fixing the heavy marble lid over the tomb. They sealed it tight, with strong mortar and heavy boulders and evil spells. She could hear Phairee laugh as the guards worked.

The blackness that settled over Clareesh then and forever was a thing the human mind cannot conceive. A nightmare that has no end. For Clareesh could not die. No matter how much her hands bled from tearing at the lid of the tomb. No matter how much moisture she lost from the tears she could not stop shedding. Her form was made of a matter the elements of the Earth could not permanently break down. She could only lie in darkness, eternal forsaken darkness, beside the rot of her dear love, and pray for the end of time.

27

Mary awoke in her bed. Sunlight, the color and texture of fog lit with headlights, flowed through her windows. She glanced at her digital clock—eight-forty. She was late for school.

Sitting up and reaching for her robe, she saw streaks of red rust on her sheets. Touching it, she was reminded of dried blood. Of gallons of sticky red liquid that had slowly evaporated in a desert tomb. She remembered her dream, then, and the little alien. Why was her robe off? She'd had it on when they locked fingers in the backyard. Had the little guy knocked her out and undressed her and put her to bed? Just before using a long silver needle to insert the burning akashic records directly into the core of her brain. God, what a torture. To never be allowed to die. Poor Clareesh. Jarteen had gotten off easy.

But it had nothing to do with her.

"It was just a dream," she whispered.

Yeah, and Tom was just the new kid on the block.
Where had he gone when he left her?
Did he have a home? Did he need one?
She was going to find out.

That day at school she carefully avoided Tom. During break she sat in her car and smoked cigarettes. At lunch she stayed in the girl's room and smoked. But right after final period, she crouched in the bushes alongside the parking lot and watched as Tom smoothly moved out across the back of the campus. Quickly she jumped in her car and followed.

He walked all over town, seemingly without a destination; not buying anything, or eating anything, or even looking at anything in particular. He moved as if in his own universe. She wondered if that wasn't the precise truth. She doubted that he saw the same city that everyone else saw. True, he stopped at intersections and all that, but the whole town seemed to be a prop to him. He was walking around on a sound stage the rest of them could not see. She wondered who the director was, if the script called for another bloody ending.

As much as she tried to push away Clareesh's tale, it plagued her in the same way that Jerry's death haunted her. She could still see in her mind's eye the first statue Jarteen had carved of Clareesh. She remembered it as something Jerry might have created.

She could still see the blood gushing from Jarteen's wounds, forming a dark puddle that spread across the bedchamber. They didn't have ballots in those days. No one had voted Clareesh to her supreme position. But it could have been Jerry's blood.

Spreading and then drying.

Waiting for another age to return to life.

All are doomed to love. All are doomed to die.

And I know. Even you. Even I.

"Must die," Mary muttered, lighting another cigarette. Tom walked into the park. He didn't look at the trees. He didn't notice the playing children. Not once did he turn around, or even turn his head to the right or left. Were his eyes open? What did they see?

Toward dark, after Mary had followed him forever, Tom made a statement. He must have known she was on his tail. On the edge of town, on a road famous for its speeding cars and squished squirrels and crushed raccoons, Tom watched as a racing car was doing triple the speed limit. The driver didn't look like a local. He didn't appear to be watching the road too closely. He ran over a fox without flashing his brake lights once. The animal was hit in midbody. Yet, miraculously, although the poor thing was flat as a jellyfish, it continued to twitch. As if trying to fight its way back to life. For obvious reasons, the sight broke Mary's heart.

Tom paused and looked over at the fox.

He moved to it and knelt beside it in the middle of the road. There was gross bone and muscle tissue everywhere. Tom didn't mind; he picked up the fox and cradled it to his chest. Against his clean white shirt. From a hundred yards down the road, Mary could see the red stains forming around his pressed pockets. Tom squeezed the fox to his heart, as if he wished the echo of his own beat to enter the dying creature, to take over and pump vitality back into its crushed limbs.

And that was what happened.

The fox reinflated, as if it were a child's blowup toy hooked up to an air pump. It licked Tom on the cheek, then carefully slipped down from his hands and walked happily into the trees. Tom watched it leave, then turned in Mary's direction and sadly shook his head. He continued his walk up the road. Mary swallowed and let him go. She had to let him go; she couldn't breathe, never mind move. But later, oh yes, but not much later, she would catch up with him and have a few words.

29

Tom wasn't at school the next day. She worried that he'd never show again. Pamela was also concerned and accosted Mary at lunch.

"You didn't sleep with him already, did you?" Pamela demanded.

"It's none of your business if I did," Mary said flatly.

Pamela was livid. "You probably did and turned him off the whole Seedmont female population. He probably left in disgust thinking you were the best this town had to offer."

"I am the best this town has to offer." She added

sweetly, "Jerry knew that. He couldn't believe what an improvement I was over you."

Pamela started to slap her but Mary was too quick. She grabbed Pamela's wrist. Pamela struggled for a few seconds—but Mary was too strong for her. Finally Pamela dropped her arm and glared.

"I wouldn't be so smug." Pamela said. "I just heard this morning that they're going to exhume Jerry's body to do more tests on it."

Mary paused. "Why?"

"Why? *You* know why."

Mary tried to act bored. "What do I know?"

"That they'll find no powder burns on Jerry's hands. He didn't struggle with the guard. Someone else did." Pamela put her face in Mary's face. "That someone was you."

Mary forced a smile. "Then I guess they're going to have to dig me up as well."

It was a joke, a sick joke, nothing more. Yet suddenly each of them backed up from the other, backed up from the stink of embalming fluid that rose up between them. Pamela made a face.

"Gross me out why don't you? Yuck! You need to brush your teeth, Mary, or else get a mouth transplant."

Mary sniffed the air. "Funny, I was thinking the same thing about you."

But it wasn't funny. And neither of them laughed.

30

It seemed an extraordinary coincidence to Mary that only a couple of days ago she had told Ken and Savey the truth about that night and now suddenly the authorities wanted to exhume Jerry's body. Leaving school after last period, Mary cornered Ken in the parking lot.

"Did you tell the police what I said?" she demanded.

"No. I swear I didn't. I was just grateful you told me the truth."

"Then why are the authorities interested in digging up your brother's body?"

Ken acted dismayed. "I don't know why. Have you spoken to Savey?"

"No. But Savey wouldn't stab me in the back by telling." She paused. "Would he?"

"Ordinarily I'd say no. But he was really upset after we left your house, more than you could realize. He didn't understand why you just didn't tell the truth."

"Do you understand?"

Ken looked at the ground. "I like to think you were in shock. That you didn't know what you were doing."

"I wasn't in shock."

He raised his head. "What happened then?"

He was confused about her behavior that night, and she, too, was bewildered. Yet bewilderment and shock aren't the same. She hadn't lost track of her senses or reasoning faculties when she walked out of the office, leaving her dead boyfriend to be found by the custodian. She had left intentionally because . . .

"There's mystery here," she said quietly. "I realize that sounds like something the Ouija board might say, but it's the best I can do to explain how I felt that night." She paused. "Everything that happened then, even the three bullets fired—none of that is set in stone."

Ken frowned. "I don't understand. Jerry's dead, we can't change that."

Mary thought of the crushed fox.

"Who knows," she muttered.

"Mary?"

She held up her hand. "I know, I sound like I'm losing it. Forget what I just said. Back to Savey and his talking behind my back. Tell me more about his being upset."

"He thinks we've carried this seance thing too far. Savey doesn't believe in the supernatural, or even in life after death. He thinks that when you're put in the ground, that's it. Ball game over."

The image was disturbing for her.

Because it had a ring of truth to it.

For her. Particularly for her.

"Is anything else bothering Savey?" she asked.

Ken was uncomfortable. "You're not stupid, Mary. You know what else is going on."

"Tom?"

"Yeah, sure. I mean, it's none of my business. It's only that the guy has just shown up and Savey says you're already screwing him."

"I haven't screwed him. That's an exaggeration."

"Like I said, it's none of my business."

"But you're implying that Savey, because he was angry with me for being with Tom, may have used what I told you the other night against me?"

Ken shook his head. "Maybe you'd better ask him instead of me."

"I'll do that," she said.

31

Mary had to go to work immediately after school, and didn't have a chance to see Savey. At the theater Mr. Barker was counting the previous days receipts. He hadn't been in the day before because he was ill. He asked Mary if she could make the popcorn and sweep up. She had seen what needed to be done and had the broom and dust pan out already.

"Seen any more flying saucers?" he asked casually as she worked.

"Just the one. It comes down every night."

He set aside a roll of quarters. "Seriously?"

"Yeah. Saw an alien last night as well. That's the second time. He's a cute little guy with huge black eyes."

Mr. Barker stared at her with his glass eyes. "There's something in your voice—you're not kidding." He paused. "You know I hear everything when a person speaks. My ears are all I've got."

"I've known that for a long time, Mr. Barker. That's why I tell you things. You know I'm not hysterical."

He asked her to sit down beside him at his desk. "Tell me everything."

"All right," she said. She told him about her walks in the woods, her telepathic telephone calls. She mentioned her regular visits to Jerry's grave, leaving out the part about *lying* on top of his grave. She also neglected to mention that she was the one who shot the guard. She trusted Mr. Barker, but all trust, she understood, should have limits. At least Mr. Barker wouldn't be jealous of her seeing Tom. She mentioned Mr. New Kid as well, but left out the part about the crushed fox. Mr. Barker may have had excellent ears, but there was no way he'd believe Tom could bring the dead back to life. Actually, when all was said and done, she gave Mr. Barker a censored report. Clareesh and Klaxtor were not even brought up. But what she did say was enough to blow the old guy's mind. When she finished, he sat silently for a minute.

"Five pennies for your thoughts," she said finally, putting a nickel in his wrinkled palm.

He smiled at the gesture. "I don't think you're lying, Mary."

"Then you must be as crazy as I am."

"Perhaps I am. I have a story for you that I've never told anyone before. It's about you, indirectly, about when you were born."

"Get off."

"Listen, then form your own opinion. It happened nineteen years ago. It was late winter—say February or early March. Like you, I was fond of hiking in the woods. I had my eyes then. I could see a fox in a tree a mile away. I still had my looks. Half the women in town were in love with me."

"The other half are in love with you now," Mary said.

Mr. Barker chuckled. "You flatter me. I know I'm a local joke. It doesn't bother me, as long as I am able to help the community in some small way. I feel this theater does that."

"I love this place," Mary said honestly. "All my friends do as well."

"Thank you. That means a lot to me." Mr. Barker took a moment to collect his thoughts. "I was out late that evening. Ordinarily I tried to get back to town before the sun set, but I lost my way. That can happen even if you've grown up around here. Some evenings the woods just seem thicker. The light started to fail and I didn't have a flashlight. There was no moon, which was half my problem. I wasn't scared, at first, just anxious. I didn't want to run into a bear, and I certainly didn't want to spend the night in the woods. It was cold. All I had on was a jacket. You can easily die of hypothermia if you're not careful. It's happened before.

"After hours of wandering around more and more worried, I stumbled across the cemetery. I hadn't been looking for it. But it was a landmark, and did give me a clear idea of where I was. But by then it was completely dark. Nineteen years ago there was no road to the graveyard, only a dirt path. A hearse couldn't get through on it. In those days, all the bodies to be buried were brought out in a small horse-drawn carriage. I know it sounds primitive but that's how it was. Ask your parents about it. I'm sure they'll remember.

"Anyway, I took one look at the cemetery, at the

untended plots and crooked rows of tombstones, and decided to get out of there as fast as possible. I wasn't superstitious. But I think it is a rare man or woman who can feel comfortable in a graveyard at night. Plus there was a feeling in the air, a certain smell—it's hard to explain, but it's at the core of what I'm getting to. Before a big thunderstorm, there's always a charge in the atmosphere. Most animals can feel it, and some people can as well. You know something big is about to happen. That any second lightning will flash and thunder will roll. Well, that night there was the equivalent of a *psychic* charge in the air. I know that sounds silly but that's the best way I can put it. Not everything in the cemetery was completely at rest. I mean, I couldn't see anything moving. I could hardly see at all in the dark. The night was one of the blackest I could remember. I couldn't see my own feet. But I knew astral lightning was about to strike, and I sure as hell didn't want it to strike me. I felt that if I didn't get out of that cemetery right then, I would be irreversibly altered."

"What do you mean?" Mary interrupted.

Mr. Barker wiped his brow. He had begun to perspire. Clearly, he wasn't making the story up. His old lids blinked over his glass eyes. Her question had disturbed him.

"I felt that there was something there. And that it needed a body."

"Were you afraid of being possessed?"

He hesitated. "Yes. I didn't want to use that word, but since you bring it up, that's exactly how I felt. Let me go on."

Mary nodded. "Please do."

"I managed to find the dirt path to town. That may not sound like much of an accomplishment, but because of the way I was feeling, and in that utter darkness, I considered myself lucky. I practically had to get down on my hands and knees to be sure I was on the path. When I was positive I almost started crying. By then I was a nervous wreck, but I wasn't weak. I never have been. I fought in Korea, and was always one of the first up any hill. I just can't exaggerate this feeling of dread in the air. It kept building and building. All I knew was that I had to get out of its path, and quick."

Mr. Barker paused to wipe his forehead once more. His voice cracked as he spoke next. "I was a hundred yards down the road when it rushed out of the ground."

"What rushed out of the ground?"

"I don't know," Barker answered. "It was like a cloud of fog, pale and white as winter snow. But it sparkled and glowed. A radioactive sand seemed to be sprinkled throughout it. In places it had a faint reddish hue, as if blood gases were pumped through its center. It condensed above one spot in the cemetery, and seemed to take on a form."

"You're talking about a ghost," Mary blurted out.

Mr. Barker had to take a breath. "I don't know. No."

"It sounds like a ghost."

"It didn't feel like a ghost."

"What do you mean? What does a ghost feel like?"

"This thing didn't feel like it had anything to do with humanity. It didn't feel like it had ever been alive. Or if it had been, it had been so long ago it had forgotten what it meant to live and breathe. I tell you, the thing was like some alien creature."

"From another world?" she asked.

"Who knows. Maybe."

"Did it feel—evil?"

Her question made him pause to hink. "When I first saw it, my original intuition was that it needed a human body to feed upon in order to solidify. That was what the charge in the air was all about—the ravenous hunger of this thing, its thirst that only living blood could satisfy. The pyschic charge saturated the woods. The entire forest seemed haunted that night. This thing was ancient. It had been underground a long time and was tired of waiting. Its time had come."

"How do you know these things?" Mary asked.

"I sensed them all."

"Is it possible it communicated these things to you?"

"I never thought of that. Maybe."

"You say it began to take form. Was it a human form?"

Mr. Barker frowned. "It was roughly humanoid. But if you were to ask me, it looked more like your alien than a normal person. It had a large head, a shrunken body."

"What happened next?"

Mr. Barker shuddered. "It saw me."

"It saw you? Did it speak?"

"No. But it knew I was there. It turned in my direction. I could see its eyes then, two huge black pits. A red glow burned in its chest and increased in intensity. I didn't know what to do. I felt doomed.

The power that radiated from it was unmistakable." He coughed. "It moved toward me."

"What did you do?"

He closed his eyes briefly. "I ran, and I think I started screaming. I don't know for sure. I was absolutely terrified and could think of nothing except getting away from it. But it kept coming."

"Did it catch you?"

"Yes."

"What happened?"

He shook his head. "I shouldn't be talking about this."

Mary was exasperated. "No way you're leaving me hanging. What happened?"

He stared at her for a moment with his empty eyes. "It caught me and froze me in midstride. I don't know how. I couldn't move, I swear, no matter how hard I tried. I could only stare at it as it went through my mind. Up close it was more horrible. Its black eyes looked as if they belonged to a witch. The red glow in its chest was like something gory that had been torn from a live victim. I could feel it inside my brain, its touch cold and calculating. It was as if it thumbed through all my mental files. The strange thing is, I knew what it was looking for."

"What?" Mary asked.

"Pregnant women. It wanted to know all the women in Seedmont who were expecting. There were only four or five that I was aware of. Each of their faces stood out in stark relief in my mind. Actually, once I realized what the creature was searching for, I tried to block the identities of the women. But it found them anyway. Yet the last female it focused on was not pregnant, at least not as far as I knew. Still, her face lingered in my mind, and I assume it did likewise in the creature's." Mr. Barker paused and lowered his head. "It was your mother, Mary."

Mary nodded. Somehow, she knew his story would lead to this revelation. "And I was born nine months after this event," she said.

He nodded weakly. "I always wondered about that."

Mary smiled. "What did you wonder, Mr. Barker?"

He shook his head. "You misunderstand me. I never thought there was anything wrong with you. I just wondered if your life and what happened that night would ever collide."

Mary considered. "This spot in the ground in the cemetery where the creature rose up—do you know where it is?"

He hesitated. "Yes."

"Is it where Jerry was buried?"

He became suddenly weary. "Why do you ask?"

"Please just answer the question."

Again he coughed. "Yes. It was the same spot."

"You said this thing had the eyes of a witch. Was it female?"

He put a hand to his head. "Oh, Mary. I should never have started this. I never thought of it in those terms. But I suppose if I were to give it a sex, I would say it was female." He paused. "How did you know?"

"It reminds me of Clareesh."

"Who's that?"

"An ancient Egyptian goddess. Never mind." She

drummed her fingers on the desk beside his change. The sound startled him. She reached out and touched his arm to calm him. He was, after all, always in the dark. His black tomb followed him wherever he was. Was his blindness because of the creature he had met in the cemetery? She added, "What did the creature do when it was through reading your mind?"

He stuttered. "I can't . . . I can't remember."

"Did it just float away?"

"I suppose."

"Did it float away in the direction of town? You don't have to lie to me, Mr. Barker. I know the answer is yes."

He hesitated. "Yes. It finally released me and drifted toward town. I never saw it again." He added, "Of course I lost my eyes shortly after that."

"How did you lose them?"

"Our esteemed mayor, Mr. Patrick Poole, threw acid in my face." He added quietly, "He caught me in bed with his wife."

Mary was astounded. "The acid was sitting there ready?"

Mr. Barker nodded. "I thought the same thing myself. The acid was awfully convenient. But maybe Poole had caught his wife in bed many times before."

"Did he go to jail?"

"No. He owns the local police and judges. He got a slap on the wrist, nothing more."

Mary sighed. "I'm sorry."

"It was a long time ago. I don't think about it anymore."

"I don't believe that but it's brave of you to say so."

Mary squeezed his arm. "Why did you tell me this story?"

He patted her hand. "I thought it would help you make sense of what you're going through. I know you haven't told me all of it. I hear that in your voice. If nothing else, I thought my story would let you know that you're not alone." He paused and sniffed. "What's that smell?"

"What smell?" she asked reluctantly.

"It smells like formaldehyde."

"I don't smell anything."

He frowned and shook his head. "I must be imagining it. I know this is completely off the subject, but do you want to work tomorrow? I'm drawing up the schedule."

Mary rose and took a step back.

She didn't want him to know the source of the odor.

Why did she smell like something embalmed?

They only did that to corpses.

"No," she said. "I need tomorrow off. It's my birthday, and I want to celebrate."

32

Mary stopped at Savey's house after work. His car wasn't parked out front. Sitting a hundred yards down the street in her own car, she waited for him to show up. But after an hour or so she grew tired. On the way home, on impulse, she swung by Pamela Poole's.

Savey's car, the same BMW he had driven to the

party the previous Friday, sat on the street beside Pamela's sporty red Porsche. Mary could only imagine how close Savey and Pamela were parked inside the house. Not that she gave a damn.

Mary lit a cigarette and drove away.

33

She found Tom where she thought she'd find him. In the clearing in the forest where she'd fallen in love with Jerry. Where she'd first seen the alien. He sat on a large rock beside a tree. Not doing anything in particular, it seemed, just waiting for her. But did he know she'd arrive with her father's pistol? She hadn't known until she loaded it and packed it at the last second, along with her flashlight. Her dad had bought the gun long before Jerry took the bullet in the brain. It was normally stored on a back shelf in her parents' bedroom closet. But she'd had no trouble finding it.

She knew how to use it. She was a pretty good shot, actually. She had already killed one man, two if she counted Jerry. It was with a steady hand and a clear conscience that she pointed the pistol and the flashlight at his head.

"I want you to bring Jerry back from the dead," she said. "I want you to do it tonight. Tomorrow's my birthday, and a girl should get to make love to her boyfriend on her birthday." She fingered the trigger. "Don't you agree, Tom?"

He appeared unconcerned for his safety. "You have

seen enough to know that would be a mistake," he said softly.

She took a step closer. "You showed me what you can do on purpose."

"Yes."

"Why?"

He sighed. "You cannot avoid a temptation unless you know what it is."

"That's not true. If you don't know about something, it doesn't tempt you."

"But you do know, Mary. You've known all along."

Her aim wavered. "What have I known?"

"That you don't belong in this world. That you have to come back."

She forced a smile. Boy, did she force it. "You're full of shit. I'm a human being. I'm not some fatheaded sack of gray potatoes like you."

He gestured to his and her present physical shapes. "You can look as you wish if you leave with me. I don't know why you still cling to the illusions of this world."

She stamped her foot. "This is my world, damnit! I am not an alien! I am not Clareesh!" Tears streamed down her face as her voice cracked. "My name is Mary. Mary Weist. I belong here."

Tom stood and shook his head. "You cannot stay. If you do, the nightmare will continue." He paused. "Haven't you suffered enough?"

She continued to weep. "All I do is suffer."

"Then you do see the uselessness of this course."

"No! All I know is that I had a boyfriend I loved and he died! Now you have to bring him back to me!"

"You don't want that, Mary."

"I do! It's all I want!"

Tom gestured for her to turn her light away, which she did. He turned and put a hand on a tree, staring up at the sky. The stars were bright. She had never seen them sparkle so. Wiping away her tears, she tried not to look at them.

"Five thousand years is a long time, even for us," he said. "Much could have been learned in that time. Many could have been helped. But since we came here, neither of us has progressed. And we can only guess at those we have hurt by our absence."

Mary spoke bitterly. "I don't give a damn about creatures in outer space. I've got problems of my own."

Tom glanced at her. "There was a time when all you did was care. You labored without rest. From world to world you traveled, always seeking for that spark of life that you could nourish to growth. You were my inspiration. The Law of Life was your god."

"It still is. Bring Jerry back to life and I'll worship him."

He shook his head. "You don't know what you're saying."

She came closer, still aiming the gun at him. "You're wrong. I don't know what *you're* saying. Yeah, I've had a few weird dreams. I've talked to a spirit on the Ouija board, and seen a flying saucer or two. So what? It's all hallucination. There are mental institutes in this country jammed with people who've experienced the same things. Don't you see, they lock people up who think they're aliens. I can't buy into that. I would be taking a step backward in my healing process."

Tom caressed the bark of the nearby tree. "But you still believe I can bring your boyfriend back from the dead?"

She paused. "Yeah. I saw what you did with the fox."

"Then you have to accept everything else. There are no miracles without Clareesh and Klaxtor in the picture."

He had a point. Not that she was willing to concede it to him. "Where did you get that stupid name anyway? At least mine has a nice ring to it. You sound like a reject robot from a bad sci-fi film."

He smiled sadly. "You gave it to me."

"Oh." She shook her gun. "Listen, I don't have all night. You have to fix Jerry."

He let go of the tree. "But he's dead."

"Yes, I know that. I was there when he died, remember? But death is nothing to you, Flaxtor, or whatever the hell your name is. You cradle Jerry to your chest like you did that fox and get his heart beating and I won't bother you again."

Tom was staring at his hands now. "Jerry's been dead a month."

"The fox had every bone and organ in his body squished. And you healed him. Don't try telling me Jerry is beyond your powers. I won't buy it."

"But the fox was alive."

"Yeah, right, and he just had a vitamin C deficiency. Let me make this real clear, Tom. If you don't bring Jerry back from the dead, I'm going to make you dead.

And I believe I can. I think, right now, you're wearing a vulnerable third density body. If I pull this trigger and a bullet goes into your head, I don't think you'll be warping your starship back to starfleet academy anytime soon." She shook the gun again. "If you've known me for five thousand years, then you know I'm not bluffing."

"Does it mean nothing to you that I've waited so long for you?"

"No. I figure you have a time machine aboard your ship."

"I don't. We don't."

She tried another tack. "Look, I know in another life we must have been friends. Maybe we were even lovers. I'm sure you love me. I believe that. But in *this* life I don't know you. You're just some weird creature from Planet X that can fix my dead boyfriend."

"If you don't love me, then why were you willing to make love to me the other night?"

Mary snorted. "That was nothing. Human beings have sex with total strangers all the time. It's part of the culture. Things have changed in the past five thousand years. Are you sure you don't have a time machine? That you just didn't get here?"

He lowered his head, as if it were heavy with the weight of many years. "No, Mary," he whispered.

A long silence ensued. "Well?" she said finally. "Are you going to bring him back to life or not?"

"It's not what you want."

"It is. I swear it is."

"No. Why don't you trust me?"

"I keep telling you, I don't know you." She put the gun directly to his head. "Believe me, please, I will not feel pain killing you. I can do it. I killed that guard and didn't shed a tear for him or his miserable family. I will do it. Unless you do what I say right now."

His face was tired. "You couldn't hurt an insect five thousand years ago."

"Being locked in a black tomb for so long ruined my pleasant disposition. I am through talking. Promise to bring him back to life or I will kill you now."

"Don't you want to know what the price of bringing him back will be?"

She hesitated. "No. I don't care. I'll pay it."

"You paid it last time."

"I will pay it again!" she screamed. She struck him on the back of the head with her gun. "Answer me! Yes or no?"

He touched his head where she had hit him. As he drew his hand away, she saw blood. He stared at it as if gazing into a crystal ball. For all she knew, he had a whole shelf of them on his starship. She bet he had at least a couple of Ouija boards. He sure knew how to manipulate them. To spell out all kinds of warnings.

But he didn't know her.

There was never a chance she would have listened to any of them.

Not if it meant losing Jerry.

"I cannot say no to you," he replied, finally wiping the blood on this shirt sleeve. "I have never been able to."

"Good." She gestured with her gun. "My car is a mile from here. We'll walk to it, and then we'll drive to the cemetery. You go back on your word, you die. It's that simple."

He turned in the direction she commanded. "You know who you remind me of now?" he said.

She nodded. "Yeah. Phairee. I don't care. I just want what I want."

"So did she. But she never got it."

She shoved him forward. "We're going to change history. Move!"

34

They were able to drive straight to the cemetery without stopping because she had already placed a pick and shovel in her car trunk. She let Tom drive. It was easier to guard him that way. It was easier to think of him as Tom. That name, Klaxtor, continued to annoy her. How did she ever fly all over the galaxy with a guy with such an annoying name? He must be lying to her about it. There was no way she was going to ask his last name. It was probably a serial number.

They parked in her usual spot.

"Get out," she ordered.

He stared at the cemetery. "Seen from the fourth level, this place is shrouded in darkness."

"That's a pity. After Jerry's alive and kicking, I promise to erect a streetlight here." She poked him in the side. "Let's get this over with quick."

Unfortunately, unearthing a coffin was not easy in late November, with the ground half frozen. Even with an alien digging. Mary knew she couldn't help because she had to guard Tom at all times. He may have had miraculous healing abilities, but he was no stronger than a jock at school when it came to shoveling dirt. He even had to stop and take breaks, to catch his breath. She watched in disgust as he leaned against the shovel handle.

"Don't you have a Stairmaster aboard your spaceship?" she asked.

He didn't quit on her, however. And after two hours of carving up the earth, the pick hit wood. Sounded like a coffin to Mary. She leapt up and shone the flashlight in the hole. There was no mistaking it. They had reached the black tomb. Tom stood on top of it. He stared up at her, the light in his eyes.

"We can stop now," he said with great feeling in his voice. He was as close to pleading as he could be. "We can leave together. Once back in fourth density, this will all seem like a bad dream. A whole universe awaits us. But open this coffin, and there will be only madness. The nightmare will never end."

His words touched her. This time she felt a sharp pain in her chest. And she knew if she just let him touch her heart with his healing hands, if she just listened to him, the pain could be gone. She believed that now, unlike before. The sight of Jerry's coffin had jarred her perspective. The only problem was that Jerry was now only inches away. She just had to open the lid. Tom had to touch him—to breathe life into him.

That was all she knew!

Her boyfriend was all she had ever loved!

Mary wiped away a tear. "I'm sorry. I really am." She shook the gun. "Clean off the rest of the dirt and open it."

"Clareesh," he began.

"Don't call me that! I won't have that name! Not

now! Not tonight! Tonight is for Jerry! Open the goddamn tomb!"

Tom shoveled away the remaining dirt.

Then he popped the lid with the pick.

The stench was incredible. In her worst nightmare Mary could not have imagined such a smell. It was as if every foul odor on the planet had been mingled together and placed inside Jerry's coffin. Clasping her nose, she had to turn away. Her eyes burned from the acidic gas. It was a miracle she didn't vomit.

But there was time for that.

Eventually Mary focused her flashlight back into the hole.

It was only then that she saw him.

Jerry. A soft moan escaped her lips.

It couldn't be Jerry.

A month is a long time for a human corpse, even for one that has been embalmed. Jerry lay on his back in the coffin. He wore the same suit he had worn to the Sadie Hawkins dance in September, the rich blue one that brought out the sky in his eyes and the sun in his blond hair. The only trouble was that Tom got dirt on the suit. A handful only, but she would have to take it to the cleaners to get it perfect again. The only other little problem was that Jerry's eyes had sunk back into his head, like liquid marbles squished by the heel of a hard boot. And his blond hair was as stiff as straw. For that matter, his whole body looked stiff. His ashen face was a mask of pain. It was a lie, all the preacher's words at all the funerals in the whole world. The dead did not rest easily.

Mary swallowed. "Lift him out of the box. Put him on the grass up here."

"Are you sure?"

"Yes. Do it quickly."

While Tom lifted Jerry from his coffin, Mary turned and vomited.

Then she reached for a cigarette and her lighter. She had only one left. After placing it in her mouth, she threw the box away. And there it lay in the earth that had covered her boyfriend all the days of his death. Marlboro Country. Come to where the flavor is. Don't mind the rotting corpse. Mary sucked in a cloud of smoke and let it scorch her lungs. The pain of the fire was a pleasure. At least it was better than watching what they were doing.

"Lay him on his back," she told Tom.

Soon, Jerry was lying out in the open.

Tom knelt beside him and took his hand. For a second she worried Jerry's arm would snap off with the sudden movement, but it just made a faint creaking sound. She stood behind Tom and peered over his shoulder. She kept her flashlight largely averted. A green mold had begun to grow on Jerry's right cheek. His left ear looked as if it were infected with a purple algae. How could she ever gaze into those once blue mirrors into his soul?

That was a small question she had forgotten to ask Tom. When Jerry's body was reanimated, would his soul be there as well? She put the mystery to Tom. He nodded reluctantly.

"His soul will return," he said.

She nodded stiffly. "That's good."

Tom glanced up at her. "You think so?"

She gestured weakly. "He's no good to me unless he's who he used to be."

Tom stared at Jerry's face. "He'll never be who he was."

Mary trembled. "But you fixed the fox perfectly."

"I told you, the fox had not been dead for a month."

Mary strained to remain calm. "Can you bring him back to life or not?"

"I can."

"Then do it," she snapped.

"Don't you want to know what his condition will be?"

She wept. "If he's alive and he's Jerry, I don't care!"

Tom leaned over and brushed at the mold on Jerry's cheek. It didn't come off. Tom spoke in a gentle voice. "You must care for him first."

Mary was bitter. "Nothing can be worse than this for him!"

Tom closed his eyes and bowed his head. "That's not true."

Staring at Jerry's moldy face, she tapped the back of Tom's skull with the barrel of her pistol. She now spoke in a gentle voice. But her words were not kind.

"Do it now, Tom, before I put you both back in the box."

Tom drew in a resigned breath. "Stand back. The vibration will be strong. It could kill you."

She began to back up. "No tricks," she warned.

As before with the fox Tom drew Jerry's body close. Indeed, Tom held him as if he were the most precious thing in the universe. Mary imagined she could hear Tom's heart beating. The process didn't take much time. As he had warned, there was a vibration in the air. Yet it was swifter than mere human heartbeats, oscillating at the upper band of hearing, a sine wave beamed to the cemetery from a dimension devoid of order. Where there were no judgments, and no morality. The vibration was Mr. Barker's haunted spirit. The unspoken sound in her nightmares. The darkness that always followed the day. It was not good or bad, it was simply inhuman. The power didn't belong to the earth. It was not supposed to be invoked. Yet it was, here, now, because it was what she wished.

Then a sound came that was audible to human ears.

A faint moaning that might have been a soft whistle if the sun were out.

It seemed to come from above, and then spread out into the cemetery.

Mary heard a faint strangled sigh.

Jerry's right leg kicked.

"Jesus Christ," she gasped.

But unfortunately Jesus had nothing to do with this resurrection. Other forces were at work here, and even if Tom were an emissary from the powers of light, he had been forced by her to disobey his most sacred laws. As both Jerry's legs began to kick, and she heard him suck in a ragged breath, she didn't know whether to cry with joy or terror. Running toward them, she did both.

"Jerry!" she cried as she knelt by his side. Tom had released his tight hold. Jerry was no longer pressed against Tom's chest, but lay cradled in Tom's arms. Jerry was in the grip of a series of spasms. Her flashlight lay in the grass, framing the scene in harsh light and shadows. His limbs continued to flail as he strained to force air into lungs that were collapsed. Mary gripped his hand. "It's me, Jerry. It's Mary. I'm right here."

For the first time, she noticed the dark hole in his forehead.

Why, of course, it was still there.

Jerry opened his eyes then, and desperately searched with what was left of his vision. But with his shrunken eyeballs, it was obvious he was completely blind. His cracked lips moved and a heartrending moan escaped from his mouth.

"Oh," he gasped.

"He's choking!" Mary snapped at Tom. "Sit him up straight."

It took both of them to get Jerry into a sitting position. Besides his continuing spasm, he was as stiff as, well, a corpse. Mary had to kneel on his back to get it to bend. The sound of his popping joints only increased her anxiety. It was possible, she thought, that she had just broken his back. Bent over, Jerry began to hack violently.

"Do something for him!" she screamed at Tom.

But Tom sat back and shook his head. Suddenly he seemed to be having trouble sitting upright himself. His voice came out weak and exhausted. "I have done too much. I can do no more. He is your problem now."

"You can't desert us now," Mary said, trying to hold on to her convulsing boyfriend. "You have to help us!"

Tom labored to breathe. "I can't."

"Why can't you?" She had dropped her gun while trying to help Jerry, but she reached for it once more. "I'll kill you if you don't help him, I swear it."

Tom smiled faintly. "You have already killed me, Mary. It took all my life energy to bring him back to life. That was one of the costs you didn't want to hear about."

Mary was astounded. "What are you going to do?"

He nodded to the open grave. "I will just sit here for a little while, say goodbye to the stars. Then I will crawl into the hole. It's best, I think."

Mary let go of the gun and patted Jerry on the back, as if he were a baby. Slowly, his hacking began to subside. But he was still in no shape to speak. And this was supposed to be a joyous moment? She felt utterly awful and confused.

"What about your spaceship?" she asked Tom. "Have it come. Don't you have a ship's doctor?"

Tom shook his head faintly. "I have no power left to bring it. And I have waited all these years for you alone." He paused to cough. "There is no doctor who can heal me now."

She was crying again. "I'm sorry." Jerry shivered violently. It was as if he were receiving constant electrical shocks from a live wire. Mary tried to hug him but the stink kept her from really holding him. "What am I supposed to do with him?" she pleaded desperately.

Tom leaned back and closed his eyes. His voice came out as if from far away. Maybe a part of him already was out in the stars.

"You can only give him love," he whispered. "Coming back to this world this way—nothing else can soothe his agony."

35

It was on the drive home that Jerry managed to speak his first recognizable words. She had him strapped tight in the seat beside her. She had thrown a blanket over all but his head. He looked terribly uncomfortable, like an ironing board crammed into a closet two sizes too small. His morbid eyes continued to search for a source of light they would never find. He smelled of putrefaction. The stink etched a permanent stain in her heart. She knew she would never be able to forget it, no matter what followed. She would never be able to have someone else in her car, no matter how many times she cleaned it. Something seemed to leak from his side, dripping into the upholstery. It was not at all like their first date.

"God," he said painfully.

Mary reached over and touched his side. "It's Mary. I'm right here."

He turned his head in her direction. His ligaments and tendons were obviously tight. His neck made a sick tearing sound as he tried to look at her. His lips labored. His jaw creaked.

"No," he moaned. "No Mary."

Her eyes were damp. "It's me, Jerry. You're back in your body. I brought you back. I'm taking you to my house. You're going to take a bath and change your clothes." She smiled bravely. "You're going to be just fine."

His hand found hers, and it was all she could do not to recoil from his touch. His fingers were like pencils that had been dipped in wax and then left to dry. He was breathing regularly now, but the air that came out of his lungs was swamp gas.

"Mary," he said, sand on his vocal cords.

"Yes, Jerry," she answered quickly. "I'm right here. What can I do for you?"

"Hurt."

"You hurt? You poor dear. I have Tylenol at the house. You can have a half dozen tablets as soon as we get there."

"Pain."

She squeezed his hand, hoping it didn't crack. "I know you're in pain. I'll get you something stronger than aspirin. I'll break into the drugstore. I'll get you morphine. You don't feel anything when you're on morphine."

He wept then, and she could never have imagined how horrible it was to see a corpse cry. Because his entire head was so dehydrated, he had no moisture to shed tears. But his mossy cheeks creased as he sobbed, and his teeth chattered together. He started to shiver again.

"No," he moaned. "No, Mary."

She was worried. "No Mary what? You don't want any morphine? I can get you Demerol." She was close to hysteria herself. "What, Jerry? Just tell me what you need. I'll get it for you."

He let go of her and touched his hands together, felt his face. His fingers came to the hole in his forehead. He fingered the torn tissue around the perimeter of the wound, no doubt remembering back to that night a month ago when a bullet had torn through the center of his brain. If possible, his ghastly expression became even more grisly. He pressed his hands over his face and let out a strangled sound.

"Why don't you let me be dead?" he cried.

That took Mary back a step. But she recovered.

"Because I love you," she said simply.

"Mary . . ."

"Shh," she interrupted softly. "You cannot be dead. I won't allow it."

36

He began to leak real bad when she had him undressed and in the bathtub. An autopsy had been performed on him when he died, naturally. There were two long incisions down his front. One stretched from his lower right ribs to his left ribs. The other cut was vertical; it ran from his pubic bone to his Adam's apple. The stitching was jagged, not tight. Coroners didn't have to close incisions with the skill of surgeons. Their patients never complained. Until now. As the embalming fluid leaked out of Jerry's abdomen into the warm bath water, he looked down in terror. His organs could have been melting on him. Briefly she wondered if he had many of those left, if the morgue hadn't thrown most of his parts away while getting him ready for his funeral. He shook like a small child.

"Mary," he cried. "It hurts."

She sponged his back. "You want another Tylenol?"

"No."

"What do you want then? You have to tell me."

"I want it to stop."

"All right," she said, pressing her sponge on the portion of the leaking incision. "I'll go get a needle and some thread. I'll sew you up better." She went to get up. He grabbed her arm.

"Don't leave," he pleaded.

"I'll be back in a second. Just hang on."

Unfortunately, for a person who had been dead for a month, he had extraordinarily sensitive skin. The moment she pierced the needle through his skin, he let out a bloodcurdling scream. He flailed in the bathtub, soaking her with water and embalming fluid. She wished she could take him to the hospital and turn him over to a doctor's care. But the only physician who could treat him was probably in Transylvania. She wrapped her arms, around him, even though he stunk as bad as ever.

"I'm sorry," she whispered in his ear. "I'm doing everything I know for you, Jerry. I've just never dealt with a situation like this before. Where does it hurt?"

Of course it was everything that hurt. But as he moaned and wept and gestured, she began to get the idea that it was the embalming fluid itself that was burning him. It was ironic because he felt cold, even in the warm water. Yet she worried about draining the fluid out of him, without first having something to replace it with. Like it or not, the formaldehyde was circulating in his system, maybe keeping him alive.

Then it hit her.

He needed blood. Fresh blood.

Mary hurried him out of the tub and dried him quickly. Wrapping him in her woolen robe, she led him into her room and tucked him in her bed. He lay shivering like someone in the grip of a fatal fever. She kissed him on his forehead near his bullet wound. She closed her eyes as she did so. The hole was wide; she could see his brains through it.

"I'm going out for half an hour," she said. "I'm going to get you something that will make you feel better. You might even be able to see again after I'm through, I'm not sure. All you have to do while I'm gone is relax. This is the bad part here, when you've just come back to life. I swear it's going to get better as time passes." She tried to make her voice sound enthusiastic. "It will be like old times. We'll go to the movies and dinner and make love all night. What do you think of that, Jerry?"

He shook his head. "No love, Mary. No."

She patted his arm. "Well, we can wait a while on the sex."

In the living room Mary picked up the phone and dialed Pamela Poole. Her old rival—and Mary was only beginning to get an idea of just how far back the two of them went—answered promptly. It was two in the morning but it did not sound as if Pamela had been asleep. Mary had to wonder if Savey would hear her talking in the background.

"Hello?" Pamela said.

"Hi, Pamela. This is Mary. I want to make you an offer you can't refuse."

"Really? Sounds intriguing. How do you plan on screwing me this time?"

"Shut up and listen. This is a serious offer. I am willing to turn over to you the *real* ballots that were cast for homecoming queen if you and Savey agree to stop pressuring the authorities into exhuming Jerry's body."

Clearly her offer took Pamela's breath away. She was a long time answering. "I can't speak for Savey. What makes you think I can?"

"You always speak for the boys you're having sex with. Why should you change now?"

Pamela laughed. "There really is another set of homecoming ballots?"

"What do you think Jerry was doing in the office that night? Checking on his grade point average?"

"What do the real ballots add up to?"

"For whom?"

"For me, you idiot."

"Let's just say you'll be pleased with the results." Mary paused. "Do you want to make the deal or not?"

"How do you know—once you turn the ballots over to me—that I'll do what you want?"

"You mean, I can't trust you?" Mary asked.

"I think our level of mutual trust is about as low as an ant's ass."

"True. I have thought of your objection. I'm not the idiot you imagine. I know you will drop the idea of me being there that night because it will cast suspicion on the validity of this new set of ballots."

Pamela was shrewd. "I think my talking will have the opposite effect."

"No. Because if you agree to leave me alone, I will drop hints at school that Jerry did in fact talk about trying to get me illegally elected homecoming queen."

Pamela was impressed. "You would really do that?"

"As long as you keep cool, I stay cool."

"But we don't control the cops. They may exhume Jerry's body anyway."

Mary noticed Pamela's use of the word *we*.

"You are the ones pressuring the authorities. Until a few days ago, they had closed the case."

"That's true." Pamela considered. "I want to see these ballots."

Mary smiled. "You can see them tonight. Meet me in front of the movie theater. Come alone. If you have anyone else in the vicinity, I'll destroy these ballots tonight."

"I'm surprised you haven't destroyed them already."

"I thought they might come in handy someday."

37

Mary arrived before Pamela. She brought her father's gun, but didn't bother fixing up a fake bag of ballots. She planned on taking Pamela out quick. Along with the gun, she had a hammer. Pamela had a hard head but tonight she was going down. Mary felt no qualms of conscience. She owed Phairee one for that black tomb number she had pulled on Clareesh back in Egypt.

Mary had not changed her clothes.

She positively stunk.

The town square was deserted. It always was at this time of night. Another reason Mary had chosen the theater as a meeting place was that it was located next to the town drugstore, which she planned to break into as soon as she had Pamela in the trunk. Mary figured she'd need sterile needles, tubes, tourniquets and flasks to hold the blood. She didn't know how much blood Jerry'd need to feel better, but she planned on giving him whatever it took.

Pamela showed up five minutes after Mary arrived. She parked her Porsche behind Mary's car and climbed out. Mary jumped out as well. Pamela was a spunky girl. She had come alone. Pamela made a face as Mary approached.

"Christ," she said. "What happened to you? You look like hell. You . . . Yuck!" She grabbed her nose. "You stink! I'm warning you, Mary, you better not have polluted the homecoming ballots. I need those to consummate my senior year."

Mary pulled the gun from her back pocket and pointed it at Pamela's head. "You won't be consummating or fornicating any more this year. Put your hands over your fat head before I put a bullet in it."

Pamela's face darkened and she sneered. "You wouldn't shoot me. You don't have the guts."

"I shot the guard. Blew his guts all over the wall. Don't push me, Pammy, I would get a lot of pleasure out of killing you."

Pamela thought about that a moment. She raised her arms. "You're not going to get away with this."

Mary took a step closer. "You'd be amazed what I've gotten away with tonight." She gestured with the pistol. "Turn around."

A note of fear entered Pamela's voice. "What are you going to do?"

"Nothing you won't find interesting. Turn now."

Pamela turned. She spoke over her shoulder. "I don't want you messing up this sweater. My father bought it for me last Christmas and it's made of cashmere. It cost over five hundred bucks."

"That should be the last of your worries right now." Mary removed the hammer from her belt. "Jerry honestly did think you were lousy in bed. He told me once after we made love." Mary raised the hammer. "He said having sex with Pamela Poole was like riding a skateboard on ice."

Pamela went to turn. "You lie. He told me that I was so hot that . . ."

Mary brought down the hammer. Pamela crumpled to the ground.

"Did he tell you that you were so hot your blood could warm him on a cold night?" Mary asked.

She took out her keys and opened her trunk.

38

Mary had no trouble breaking into the drugstore and collecting the supplies she needed. She picked up some morphine while she was at it. She could dissolve the pills in a glass of water, she thought, and make him sip them down. She had already given him one glass of water, successfully. Yet she had to wonder if Jerry's digestive system really worked. To be frank, he hadn't been to the toilet in a long time. She prayed to God he had no huge worm crawling around in his intestines.

On the drive home, with Pamela rolling from side to side in the trunk, Mary's thoughts turned to Tom. She felt bad about having left him by the grave, especially after he had waited five thousand years for her. But she didn't know what else she could have done. She didn't understand why he couldn't call for help, despite his explanation. There was supposed to be a deluge of flying saucers all over planet Earth, if you believed what the tabloids had to say, which she was more inclined to do these days.

Before getting Pamela out of the trunk, she checked on Jerry. He wasn't a lot better. He was still shivering and his pain appeared all but intolerable. She showed him the bottle of morphine before remembering he couldn't see. She tried to sound cheery.

"I got some stuff that gives you the coolest high. I'll grind up a few tablets and in a few minutes you'll be floating."

He stared in her direction with his sunk eyeballs. His speech seemed to be improving, if nothing else. Not that she liked what he had to say.

"I was floating," he said.

Mary froze. "Before I brought you back?"

"I was happy."

"Where were you?"

He looked so sad. "I can't remember now. But I was happy."

"But aren't you happy to see me? I mean, to be with me again?"

He took a long time to answer. "I was dead. I should be dead."

"You have to stop thinking that way. I've gone to a lot of trouble to bring you back to life. You have to look at the bright side. This isn't such a bad place to be. You can start sculpting again. Why, I'll even pose nude."

He glanced down at his hands. "I cannot see. All I can feel is pain." A tear ran over his moldy cheek. The glass of water must have done him some good, after all, if he could cry real tears. "I want to die, Mary."

She quickly stood back from the bed. "I am not going to listen to that kind of talk. Life is a gift that you can't lightly throw away. Besides, we're going to do a little experiment. We're going to give you a series of transfusions. I bet you ten bucks it puts color back in your cheeks." She noticed how green his mold was. "I mean, a rosy color."

"Where did you get the blood?"

She paused. "At the hospital."

He shook his stiff neck. "They did not give you blood."

"Don't worry about it. Just enjoy it." She turned away. "I'll be back."

39

Pamela regained consciousness while Mary was tying her into a chair in the garage. Mary had already placed a strip of strong adhesive tape over Pamela's mouth so she was not worried about the cheerleader calling out for help. Mary preferred to keep her blood supply in the garage so as not to upset Jerry. His mood was obviously sensitive at the moment.

Pamela's eyes grew wide when she saw Mary carefully arranging the tourniquets, needles, plastic tubing, and flasks on a nearby stool, that Mary had earlier covered with a clean pillowcase. Mary felt that she owed Pamela a partial explanation since she was probably going to take so much of her blood that the girl's heart would stop beating.

"I guess you're wondering what your old friend is up to tonight," Mary said. "To be honest, you're not going to believe what I have to say. Nor are you going to like it. But in a way you started it all with your silly seance. You see, that spirit we spoke to on the Ouija board was really an alien named Klaxtor. He's been hanging around this planet for several thousand years, hoping to talk me into returning with him to outer space. Oh, I forgot to mention, I'm an alien, too. Don't ask me what star I'm from, though. I haven't the foggiest. I got trapped here in ancient Egypt when I tried playing the high goddess. Back then I had this friend named Phairee—who was you in a past life—

who caught me in bed with Jarteen—who was Jerry in a past life. Phairee was as vain as I was about her looks. Her problem was that she wasn't an alien, so she kept getting older and older, and grew more and more resentful of myself. When she caught me in bed with Jarteen, she saw a chance to blackmail me. She demanded that I make her immortal. But I couldn't do that because it was against this thing called the Law of Life, and beside I didn't know how to do it anyway. To make a long story short, you locked me in a black tomb with my dead lover and I was stuck there practically forever. And now I'm going to repay your favor. Oh, wait, another thing. That new kid at school, Tom, is really Klaxtor. He's already brought Jerry back from the dead. Yeah, isn't that incredible? Right now Jerry's lying in my bed. But he's in bad shape. He looks like shit and he's in terrible pain. He needs blood—that's what I think—and since you cut him open last time and he bled like crazy, I think the karma of the situation demands that I take your blood and give it back to him." Mary picked up a needle and tourniquet and grabbed Pamela's arm. "Hold still, my dear. This won't hurt a bit."

Pamela did not take her advice about holding still, but since Mary had already tied her wrists to the arms of the chair, the cheerleader's lack of cooperation was academic. Mary applied the tourniquet and found a plump vein and pretty soon her flasks were filling nicely. Pamela wore the funniest expression on her face as she stared at the dark blood. It made Mary laugh.

"I'm sorry. I made up that thing about another set of ballots. I just wanted to get you out of your house so

I could hit you over the head with my hammer. I was voted queen by a landslide. What's really incredible is that most of the guys you slept with voted against you. Really, you must be dreadful in the sack. I'm not trying to be insulting. I tell you this as a friend, one girl to another. In your next life, Pammy, try to work on that."

Mary threw her back and laughed.

She knew she was close to losing her mind.

It had been a hard night.

And it wasn't over yet.

40

While Mary was draining Jerry's stale yellow embalming fluid and refilling him with fresh red blood, Savey and Ken stopped by. They knocked before coming in, thank heaven for small favors. Cautioning Jerry to remain silent, she met them at the door smelling like the local undertaker. They both took a step back on the porch.

"Mary!" Savey cried. "You stink!"

"Thank you. I'm out of deodorant. What can I do for you?"

"Mary," Ken said in a calm voice, although he was also clearly shocked at her appearance. She hadn't cleaned up since being at the cemetery. "What is going on with you?"

"Nothing. What are you guys doing here in the middle of the night?"

"We're looking for Pamela," Savey said.

"You're looking here?" Mary tore into him. "You have a lot of nerve. Last Friday you said that you felt 'a physical necessity to make love to me.' Like you would die if you didn't. You did everything you could to get my clothes off. Then when I did undress, you massaged my naked butt for half an hour while totally ignoring my sore calves. You told me you loved me. Then, tonight, I just happen to drive by Pamela's house and I see your car parked out front."

"I stopped by to lend her a CD," Savey said defensively.

"Ha! You wanted to lend her information. By strange coincidence, right after I opened my heart to you that night, the police wanted to dig Jerry back up and reexamine his bones." She glanced over her shoulder in the direction of her bedroom. "Well, I swear to you, it's not going to happen."

Savey was unmoved. "You have it all wrong." He caught another whiff of her and backed up farther. "But I can't explain it to you now. Mary, please, why do you smell like embalming fluid?"

"How do you know what embalming fluid smells like?" she snapped back.

Savey and Ken exchanged worried glances. "Have you seen Pamela?" Ken asked carefully.

Mary tried to fix her hair. "No."

"That's odd," Savey said. "Her parents say she left home an hour ago. On the way out, she told them she was going to meet you."

"A likely story," Mary countered. "Why would I want to meet Pamela in the middle of the night? I'm one of the few people in town who isn't sleeping with her. Besides, what are Pamela's parents doing up so late that they know their daughter is sneaking out? I don't believe a single word of your story." She eyed Savey suspiciously. "Were you there when I called?"

He fidgeted. "No."

"Liar! Her parents didn't tell you anything. Her mother and father wouldn't know if Pamela didn't come home for a week. They're all sluts in that house. They prowl the streets ceaselessly. For them it's always mating season. You were there when I called, Savey, admit it."

He was offended. "What if I was? That's none of your business. We're not lovers. You hold out on me because of your deep grief over Jerry. That's what you say. But a new guy shows up on campus and you can't get into his pants fast enough."

Mary sulked. "He's not a new guy. He's really a very old friend."

Ken spoke diplomatically. "It sounds like you two are having a communication breakdown. I don't care about that. I am just concerned about you, Mary. And I am curious where Pamela is."

Mary wiped her sticky fingers on her pants. "Thank you, Ken, for your concern. I am going through a rough patch is all. Now I was just going to take a shower and wash my hair and go to bed. I don't know where Pamela is. I don't care if she has flown off to an exotic country with an international playboy, or if her body is ever found." She began to close the door. "Now if you two will excuse me . . ."

Savey blocked the door. "Her car is parked in front of the drugstore where you said you'd meet her."

Mary was annoyed. "Do you, like, bug people's phones or what? How do you know all this crap?"

"She told me," Savey said.

Mary threw her hands in the air. "She told you! And you believe her! Really, Savey, I think you've moved a step down from the Chester twins. At least they're innocent. Too stupid to know when a guy like you is taking advantage of them." She tried closing the door again. "Now I've got to get this hair dye out of my hair before I faint from the fumes. Good night boys."

She shut the door. It remained shut.

Jerry was making noise in the bedroom.

Mary hurried to his side. The blood was not helping much. His coloring was still lost somewhere between a month-old corpse and a two-month-old corpse. Maybe she needed to give him large transfusions. Pamela was probably good for another three or four pints. The cheerleader was still alive in the garage—at last check—but she had definitely lost her cheerleader sparkle. Mary took Jerry's right hand and caressed it between her palms. She ended up rubbing off a couple of layers of skin. Jerry stared at her with morose dead eyes.

"Was my brother here?" he asked, his words finally clear.

"Yes. But I didn't think you wanted to have visitors right now."

"I can't see my brother in this condition. It would kill him."

"I suppose later would be better."

"Was Savey here?"

"Yes."

"What did they want?"

"Just to chat."

"Isn't it the middle of the night?"

"Yeah. We've all been keeping weird hours since you were shot. Holding seances and stuff like that in the early morning hours."

"What do you do?"

"We use a Ouija board and light candles and try to talk to you."

"I was gone, Mary."

She bit her lip. "I know. It was just, you know, so hard that I couldn't see you anymore." She choked back the feelings. "I couldn't bear it. I just wanted to die."

He squeezed her hand. "I understand." He seemed to ponder her remarks for a few moments, and in those moments it was as if her old Jerry was back in the room. He was no longer moaning and carrying on. Perhaps the blood had done him some good, after all. Yet it was more than that. For the first time since digging him up, she could really feel him, feel his soul perhaps. His mouth twitched; the purple lips worked. He might have been trying to smile, to give her comfort. He spoke in a kind tone. "How did you bring me back?"

"I met an alien. This guy at school. He can raise people from the dead."

Jerry definitely smiled. Too bad she saw his teeth. He needed dental work in the worst way. He had more cavity than gum tissue. "Tell me about it," he said.

Mary told him the whole story, the complete and uncensored version. All the close encounters, all the nightmares. Before she was finished, she was crying again. But she managed to take him up to the point where he woke up in the cemetery.

"I just couldn't let you go," she wept. "I'm sorry."

He squeezed her hand again, held it this time. Then he took it and placed it on her heart. "Can you feel it beating?" he asked.

She frowned. "No. What's wrong with your heart?"

"I think it's been cut out."

"Then how can you be alive?"

He shook his head. "That's it. This is not life. Your friend has great power. He drew me back from a distant place. He gave my body some ability to move, to act. But he could not take away the pain of my decaying flesh. He is able to fight death but he cannot conquer it." Jerry pressed her hand against his cracked lips. He spoke to her as he used to, when he was alive. When he used to tell her how much he loved her, and how he would always be with her. The tone was the same, only the words were different. "I have to go back, Mary. You have to let me go."

She could not breathe. How could she answer him?

"I can't," she whispered.

"You must. I was somewhere before I returned. A beautiful place. There is life after death. This I know for sure now. If I leave you now, it doesn't mean I will never be with you in the future."

But she shook her head. "You did not listen close enough to my story. I am not like you. I am not from this place. I will not go the same place when I leave here. I am only bound to humanity through you. You're my only link. If you go, I am nothing. Dust floating between the stars." She lowered her head and wept on his thigh. "We will never meet again, in this world or in the next."

He patted her hair. "You don't know that for sure. No one knows what God has planned."

She sat up. "God did not raise you from the dead. I did."

He nodded. "Then you must kill me."

Her question was a tear in her soul. "Again?"

"It wasn't your fault."

"Yes, Jerry. From long ago, it was all my fault."

He sighed. "Will you do it?"

She kissed his hand. "I will do it. For you."

41

Mary half expected to find a dead alien lying beside the grave. She had thought because Tom's powers were all used up, he would not have the strength to maintain his illusion of humanity. But when they got to the cemetery she saw that she had it backward. He was still Tom. He lay near the hole, his feet dangling slightly over the edge. He was so weak he no longer had the capacity to get out of his third density body. Yet he sat up as they approached. She could see him in the beam of her flashlight. He actually waved. Perhaps he had expected them to come back.

Before leaving the house, she called the hospital to come for Pamela.

Bring plenty of blood, she had told them.

Pamela was tough. She'd live.

Jerry leaned heavily on her right shoulder. He couldn't walk without her help. When they had reached the grave, however, he was able to stand on his own at the edge of the hole, sort of, as long as she held on to one arm. Jerry stared down at Tom, and the dead man and the dying alien exchanged long looks. What had the two shared when their life rhythms had been briefly linked? Mary could only imagine.

"I'm sorry you gave up so much for nothing," Jerry said finally.

Tom spoke in a hoarse tone. "I did what my goddess wished. I cannot have any regrets." He gestured to her. "Do you have any?"

She nodded. "That is all I have."

Because she did not want Jerry to suffer.

Because she could not say goodbye again.

Because there was no hope.

Because she loved him.

Mary withdrew the pistol she had hidden in her coat pocket and jammed it at the base of Jerry's skull. Before he could react, or even know what she intended, she pulled the trigger. Yeah, she shot the love of her life—of many lives—in the head. For the second time, some cynics might say. It was even possible the fresh bullet struck the old one, if the coroner had not removed it. For sure, she shot him on the opposite side of the head. The bullet probably found the path of the other piece of lead. The path of least resistance. But she was happy it did not emerge out the other side.

She was just relieved it did its job.

THE VISITOR

Jerry toppled dead into his grave.

Her boyfriend. Gone, just like that.

Life was a mystery. But death was no solution.

Mary dropped the gun and hung her head.

A moment of silence, of respect for the dead, went by.

"That was brave of you," Tom said finally.

Her throat was dry. She could hardly speak. Her soul was a desert. She did not want to feel. Yet the pain was as sharp as always. The desert was vast. Five thousand years and she had failed to cross it. How could she ever think of reaching the stars? It was not possible, in this life or the next.

Something swept over her right then.

Unexpected. A vibration. A higher authority.

She felt power in her spine. It moved up toward her skull.

Suddenly she knew things.

For example, she intuited a point in space far beyond the borders of the universe, where the galaxies collided and new dimensions were born in the centers of black holes. Here all relative matter was crushed. It was a cauldron of destruction and a wellspring of creation. She actually saw this place, even as she stood in the dark cemetery, and felt its importance in the overall scheme of things. It was alien to her limited human mind, and yet it was the most poignant of all spots. Just the memory of the cosmic womb filled her with overpowering nostalgia.

It was so far away.

She remembered all of Clareesh's journeys with Klaxtor.

She knew she was late, too late, to return to this home.

"I learned bravery too late," she mumbled.

"Better late than never." Tom nodded toward the hole. "You will have to bury both of us. Then call for the ship. It's the only way."

He did not see the transformation in her. Curious. She shook her head. "No."

"Mary."

She raised her head and a bitter smile touched her lips. "Have you forgotten? My name's Clareesh. I am still your commander. I still have the authority to order you where I wish." She tried to raise her gaze toward the sky but it refused to go. She could only stare into the grave where Jerry had fallen. She spoke the darkest truth of all. "It is only now I realize that I never left the place Phairee buried me. All these dreams and events I have experienced are nothing. My childhood memories are frozen images washed by fire. They melt into nothingness. They are mere phantoms. I was never born. How can I die?" An agonizing wave of despair swept over her. She felt pain at the tip of each of her fingers. The blood there never really dried. The marble lid was hard. The walls of the coffin were thick. She was still trying to claw her way out. She added, "I am still there in the black tomb. Imprisoned to the end of time."

Tom protested. "You're alive now. You can leave. You have the chance."

She shook her head. "I am trapped."

"Why?"

"Because I am not Phairee. I have behaved like a

lunatic since emerging here eighteen or nineteen years ago. I have hurt people, betrayed them, lied to them. But I have never killed anyone. Because of who I am, that is one thing I would never do. I remember many things right now, Klaxtor. You would be amazed. I look like a teenage girl but I am ancient. These things come back to me like a flood of inspiration. The flood drowns me and I can hardly draw fresh air into my lungs. But I welcome it. Maybe I have earned the knowledge. Perhaps I passed some kind of test by killing Jerry. It doesn't matter. My dreams and waking have finally met. Above all else, I know the Law of Life forbids the taking of another life." She paused and nodded to him. "I cannot leave you here to die."

Tom was guarded. "Nothing can prevent my death now."

She shook her head. "You do not fool me, brave soul. You gave your life energy to raise Jerry. I can give you mine so that you may leave this unhappy world. You will call the ship, not I." She nodded at her feet. "My place is in the tomb. I am used to it."

Tom tried to stand but lacked the strength. "I do know the things you say. I have vision as well. But you were brought here—from your confinement—for a reason. You lived the life of a young woman so that you could once more live the life of a great being. Clareesh, please, you have suffered too long. You cannot throw this chance away."

She spoke the hard truth. "I have already thrown it away. When I forced you to raise Jerry from the dead. You know that as well as I. There is only one of us who can leave. It must be you. You who have remained true to your destiny." She added sadly, "While I have forsaken mine."

He stared at her in wonder. "I cannot change your mind?"

She circled the grave and knelt by his side. "No. But you can kiss me goodbye. That way my prana, my life energy, can enter your body. You know this young woman lied to you when she said she was willing to make love to you because all humans in this age are simply sex starved. She was more discriminating than that. Although confused at the time, she wanted to be with you because she loved you. She still does." She leaned over to kiss him farewell. "Please don't forget me."

He promised her that he would not.

She kissed him goodbye. Such a long goodbye.

#

She lay on her back in perfect darkness inside the coffin beside the dead body of Jerry Rickman. Far above, through the six feet of earth and the mile of sky that separated her from her ancient companion, she sensed the white light of the starship as it slowly receded into the night sky. He was finally going home and she wished him well on his long journey. He deserved to return, she did not. She accepted that. In a sense, she was in the only home that could contain her.

The dead body beside her turned to red dust.

THE VISITOR

The wooden lid above her changed to smooth marble.

She had spoken the truth.

This was the black tomb.

She had never really left.

She sighed and closed her eyes.

Mary Weist had been a dream, nothing more.

Epilogue

The seance was to be held in the library. At the last minute the Chester twins, Radi and Tori, produced a crystal ball to sit beside the Ouija board. The sudden appearance of the ball made Jerry realize that this seance had been planned long in advance. He questioned Savey about this, but his old friend said he hadn't known anything about it.

Pamela had added wicked touches to the library. There were candles and sticks of incense, plus a foot-high copper pyramid, which Pamela said she had bought in a New Age shop the previous summer. This she placed on a nearby stool, adjacent to the oak table, beside a bunch of candles. Glistening in the orange light, the copper reflected beautiful colors all around the room.

"Are you excited?" Radi asked.

Jerry forced a smile. "Yeah. I always love a seance."

Radi smiled. "You think she'll come?"

He shrugged. "I don't know."

Tori joined in. "How will we know if it's really Mary?" she asked.

"She could spell out her name," Radi suggested.

"I hope she tells us something that only Mary could know," Tori said.

"If only Mary knows it, then none of us will," Savey observed.

"God," Tori said. "That's right."

Jerry wished he was somewhere else.

"We'll know it's Mary by the way she talks," Radi said.

"She's not going to talk," Tori said. "She's just going to spell out words."

"Mary always was a real good speller," Radi said.

"Mary was always an excellent speller," Jerry corrected.

"Does this Ouija board come with a spell check?" Savey asked Ken.

Why was he putting herself through this, Jerry asked himself as Pamela finished lighting the candles and sat down at the oak table with the rest of them. If he had half a brain left, he would call a cab or walk home.

Yet Jerry stayed. The whole thing was stupid, but there was a small part of him that prayed that it worked. And there was a larger part of him that was terrified that it would.

Jerry had his reasons. Too many of them.

The lights were turned off. They had only candlelight.

"Now," Pamela began. "I have used this before, and it can blow your mind, or it can piss you off. If we screw around, the board screws with us. But if we're serious about what we're trying to do, we might get a serious response."

"What kind of responses have you gotten in the past?" Savey asked.

"They've been very interesting," Pamela said.

Jerry looked over at her. "So you've tried this before?"

"I never tried to contact Mary before," Pamela said quickly.

Jerry was annoyed at his old girlfriend. "You just asked to speak to any recently dead friends?"

"Like I said," Pamela replied, "if you have a bad attitude, it wrecks the whole thing." She paused. "Loosen up, Jerry. Relax. It's just for fun."

Jerry brushed back his blond hair and reached for the planchette. "Let's get this over with," he grumbled.

"Just a second," Pamela said, lifting a pad of paper and a pen from the floor. "We need a scribe. Someone to write down what is spelled."

There were no volunteers, except for Radi, who didn't count because she couldn't spell. In the end Pamela was forced to keep track of what was printed out. The rest of them placed their fingertips on the planchette.

"Just close your eyes and relax," Pamela whispered.

Jerry closed his eyes and sat for a minute or two, feeling nothing. Yet, suddenly, ever so slightly, the planchette began to move.

"Who's doing this?" Radi asked. "Is it you, Tori?"

"No," Tori said. "I think it's moving by itself."

"It is," Pamela said. "Open your eyes, all of you, and relax. Let it do what it wants to do for a few minutes before asking it any questions."

What it wanted to do, Jerry saw, was to move

around in larger and larger circles. But finally the planchette slowed to a crawl. It pointed at *Yes.*

"It's asking what we want to ask," Pamela said. "Is someone there?"

It moved away from the *Yes,* then returned sharply.

"Wow," Radi said. "It can hear us."

"Shh," Pamela said. "It's better to have one person talk. Otherwise, you confuse the energies." She paused. "Who's there?"

The planchette jumped to the letters.

S . . . O . . . M . . . E . . . O . . . N . . . E . . .

"Someone," Pamela muttered, as she wrote down the word. "Does this someone have a name?"

The planchette swung between *Yes* and *No.*

"Could you be more specific?" Pamela asked.

No.

"Where are you?" Pamela asked, still taking notes.

In a dark place.

"Do you want to be with us?"

No.

"Why then do you speak with us?"

I am drawn.

"Does one of us draw you?" Pamela asked.

Yes.

"Just one of us?" Pamela asked.

Yes.

"Which one of us draws you here?"

Mystery.

"Do you know who draws you here?" Pamela persisted.

Yes.

"Would you rather not tell us?"

Yes.

"Because it could upset this person?"

Yes.

"Do you care about this person?"

Yes.

"It is your care for this person that draws you here?"

Yes.

"Do care about the rest of us?"

No.

"Are you human?"

No.

"Are you dead?"

Yes.

"Were you ever human?"

Yes.

"How long ago were you human?"

Long time ago.

"Did you live in a particular country that we know of?"

Yes.

"What country was that?"

Egypt.

"You were alive in ancient Egypt?"

I was a goddess.

"Wow," Pamela said. "Were you a real goddess?"

No.

"You were a fake?"

Some might have said so.

"Do you experience emotions?" Pamela asked.

Sometimes.

"Can you experience fear?"

Yes.

"You can be afraid for us?"

Yes.

"Are you afraid now for us?"

It hesitated. A long time.

No. There is nothing to be afraid of anymore.

Pamela glanced at Jerry.

"Do you know Mary Weist?" she asked suddenly.

It hesitated.

No.

The seance ended. The Ouija board would say no more.

The group was disappointed.

Jerry was relieved. Mary was dead.

It was better to leave her that way.

Yet after Savey dropped Jerry back home, Jerry found it impossible to sleep. Not for the first time in the last month, he climbed into his car and drove out to the cemetery where Mary was buried. The place was cold and dark but he brought a warm coat and a powerful flashlight. He knew the terrain. He found her plot without difficulty.

He sat beside her grave and wept.

He remembered all too vividly that night a month earlier.

He should have told her no, they could not break into the office to count the ballots.

But he had never been able to say no to Mary Weist.

Mary had been basking in the glow of being voted homecoming queen when the light snapped on overhead and they both saw the guard with the semiautomatic pistol.

"Put your hands over your head," he said. "Slowly get to your feet."

Mary snorted. "Put down that gun. We go to school here."

The guard was scared. "You just do what I say," he whispered.

"Do what he says," Jerry told Mary, raising his own hands.

Mary threw down the ballots and climbed to her feet. She refused to put her arms in the air. The guard took a step closer. She nodded toward his pistol.

"Better put that thing away," she warned. "It doesn't look like you know how to use it."

The guard shook the weapon at her. "Put up your hands."

"No," she said.

"Mary," Jerry pleaded. "Do what he says."

"Put up your hands," the guard repeated one more.

Mary sneered. "Make me, tough guy."

To Jerry's immense surprise, the guard stepped forward and poked Mary in the belly with the barrel of his pistol. Jerry was furious. Mary doubled up in pain.

"Hey," Jerry swore. He stepped forward to push the guard aside. But he never made it. The guard turned and shot him in the right arm. He only scratched him but the sound of the bullet and the sharp pain gave Jerry reason to pause. He glanced down. His arm was bleeding. He could hardly believe it. The guard also looked shocked. He stood dumbly pointing his pistol at Jerry.

Mary went nuts, totally. She jumped the guard.

They landed in a pile and the gun went off again. There was an explosion of glass and light, and they were plunged into darkness. They rolled on the floor and she scratched at his face. The guard tried to bring the gun up but she grabbed his arm with both hands and leaned over and bit his wrist. Jerry reached down to pull them apart, when the guard screamed in pain and shoved Mary away.

The gun went off again.

Mary stopped and slowly rolled over on her back.

She had taken a bullet in the right temple. Blood soaked the floor. Jerry let out a pitiful moan. He reached down and grabbed the gun from the startled guard. He pointed it at the man's head. In the grim shadows cast by the poor light, he saw the guard shake with terror.

"Please don't shoot," the man begged. "I have a wife, a baby daughter."

Jerry put his finger on the trigger.

"Please?"

But he could not take a person's life.

Jerry dropped the gun and knelt beside Mary.

"Mary," he whispered, putting his hand over her wound. Incredibly her eyes were open; she was still alive. She looked at him with surprise. She didn't even seem to know she was hurt, although her lower body twitched with spasms.

"Jerry," she said. "Are you all right?"

He wept. "Yes. I'm fine."

"Good." She closed her eyes and drew in a deep breath. When she opened them again, she saw the blood on the floor, how it spread away from her head.

Realization crossed her face. She spoke with difficulty. "I don't feel so good, Jerry."

He held her right hand, getting his blood all over it. "You've been hurt, that's why. You take it easy. I'll call for a doctor." He froze. "Mary? Mary!"

Her eyes sank into the back of her head. Not only that—it was as if her whole face was being sucked up into some weird chasm. Her lips twisted and the flesh on her cheeks shriveled. Suddenly his eighteen-year-old girlfriend was a mummy. Her eyes briefly reappeared and she stared at him with bloodshot eyes. Her voice, as she spoke, chilled him to the bone.

"Jarteen," she whispered. "We're still in the black tomb. We're still together."

Then she closed her eyes. Her face returned to normal.

And she died, his Mary died.

"No," he pleaded. "No."

But no one was listening. She was gone.

That Saturday night, she was crowned homecoming queen.

In absentia. They had counted the ballots, after all.

Even the bloody ones.

"Oh, Mary," Jerry wept as he sat beside her grave. "I wish I was in that black tomb with you. I just wish we were together."

A vow spoken in haste is often repented in leisure.

The moment was pregnant with destiny.

A shooting star passed overhead.

Or else it was the light of a departing saucer.

Sometimes wishes could come true.

Far below him, underneath the dirt, Jerry heard a moan.

He leapt to his feet, shaking in terror.

"Mary?" he gasped.

He waited. But he did not hear the sound again.

It was late and it was cold. He was beginning to imagine things. Jerry turned to leave the cemetery. But as he did the beam of his flashlight caught on an empty box of cigarettes. It lay in the dirt at the edge of her grave and he knelt and picked it up. Come to Marlboro Country. He couldn't imagine who would have sat at Mary's grave smoking. She had never smoked in her life.

Jerry left the cemetery in a hurry.

Behind him, there came another faint moan.

He didn't hear it. Not this time.

But it would be there, another night, when he returned.

Sometimes the wrong wishes came true.

Look for Christopher Pike's

The Starlight Crystal

Coming mid-January 1996

About the Author

CHRISTOPHER PIKE was born in Brooklyn, New York, but grew up in Los Angeles, where he lives to this day. Prior to becoming a writer, he worked in a factory, painted houses, and programmed computers. His hobbies include astronomy, meditating, running, playing with his nieces and nephews, and making sure his books are prominently displayed in local bookstores. He is the author of *Last Act, Spellbound, Gimme a Kiss, Remember Me, Scavenger Hunt, Final Friends,* 1, 2, and 3, *Fall into Darkness, See You Later, Witch, Die Softly, Bury Me Deep, Whisper of Death, Chain Letter 2: The Ancient Evil, Master of Murder, Monster, Road to Nowhere, The Eternal Enemy, The Immortal, The Wicked Heart, The Midnight Club, The Last Vampire, The Last Vampire 2: Black Blood, The Last Vampire 3: Red Dice, Remember Me 2: The Return, Remember Me, 3: The Last Story, The Lost Mind,* and *The Visitor* all available from Archway Paperbacks. *Slumber Party, Weekend, Chain Letter,* and *Sati*—an adult novel about a very unusual lady—are also by Mr. Pike.